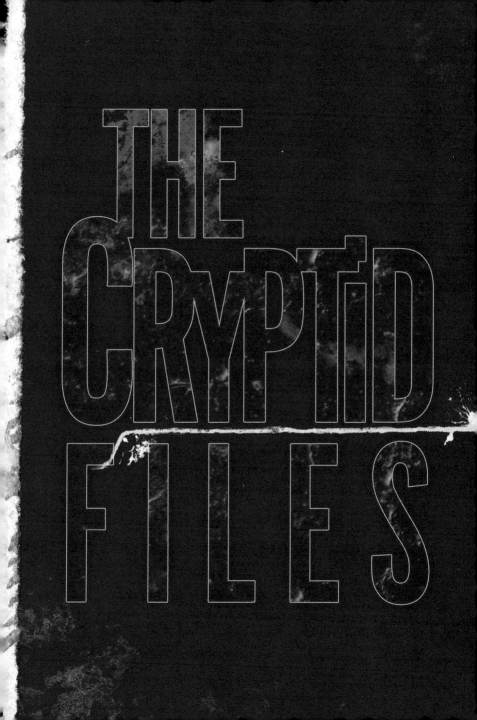

THE CRYPTID FILES

#2
THE CHUP

ACABRA

JEAN FLITCROFT

MINNEAPOLIS

First American Edition published in 2014 by Darby Creek, an imprint of
Lerner Publishing Group, Inc.

Copyright © 2011 by Jean Flitcroft

First published in Dublin, Ireland in 2011 by Little Island as The Cryptid
Files: *Mexican Devil* by Jean Flitcroft

Darby Creek
A division of Lerner Publishing Group, Inc.
241 First Avenue North
Minneapolis, MN 55401 USA

For reading levels and more information, look up this title at
www.lernerbooks.com.

Front cover: © Cynoclub/Dreamstime.com.

Main body text set in Janson Text LT Std 12/17.
Typeface provided by Linotype AG.

Library of Congress Cataloging-in-Publication Data

Flitcroft, Jean.
        [Mexican Devil]
        The Chupacabra / by Jean Flitcroft.
            pages   cm. — (The cryptid files ; #2)
        Summary: "Vanessa's summer holiday on a ranch in Mexico is turned
    upside down as she enters a shadowy world of mysterious animal death,
    magical curses and dark family secrets. As she tumbles headlong into the
    mystery of El Chupacabra she starts to understand why some call it the
    Mexican Devil"—Provided by publisher.
        ISBN 978–1–4677–3265–9 (lib. bdg. : alk. paper)
        ISBN 978–1–4677–3484–4 (eBook)
        [1. Chupacabras—Fiction. 2. Mexico—Fiction. 3. Horror stories.]
    I. Title.
    PZ7.F65785Ch 2014
    [Fic]—dc23   2013024084

Manufactured in the United States of America
1 – SB – 12/31/13

DuBOIS

To Ian, the love of my life.

CRYPT*O*ZOOLOGY

A cryptid is an animal that some people claim to have seen and which may exist in nature but which has not been accepted by modern science. Scientists who study these creatures are called cryptozoologists. This comes from the Greek word *kryptos*, meaning hidden, and zoology, meaning the study of animals.

The first book in this series is about the Loch Ness monster. In this book it's the Chupacabra—a creature in Mexico that prowls at night, drains the blood of other animals to survive, and has the eyes of the devil.

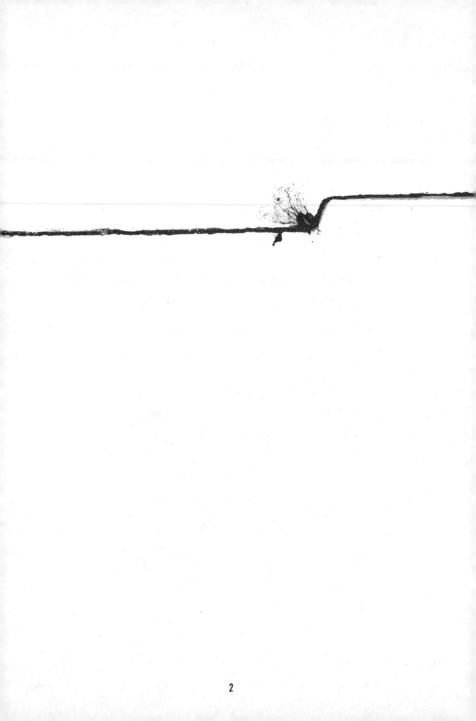

PROLOGUE

The air was thick, the heat intense, and Vanessa felt beads of sweat rise like blisters on her skin. She stumbled on into the dark, her hands outstretched as she blindly fingered the air. As she moved, cactus spines scratched her leg and a stone jabbed painfully into the sole of her bare foot. Maybe she should go back, she thought.

Something snuffled and grunted nearby, and insects clacked and ticked all around her. In the dark Vanessa struggled to make sense of the sounds and then, through it all, she heard a terrible, high-pitched squeal. She stopped suddenly, her legs like lead weights. She probably wouldn't be able to run away even if she tried.

There was something behind her now. The cracking of a small twig sounded like a gunshot in Vanessa's ears. She turned slowly, forcing herself to look. At first she thought she saw a human face, a face that she knew. But the harder she stared, the farther the face retreated into darkness and another one took its place.

Vanessa found herself looking straight into a large, salivating mouth with razor-sharp fangs. Above it two glowing red eyes pulsed to the sound of her heart, which pounded in her chest.

Too shocked to scream, Vanessa took off. She didn't feel the cactus tearing her skin this time or the cuts on her knees when she fell. She got up and kept running. Another high-pitched squeal just in front of her finally made her stop. The anguish in the cry echoed her own pain, and her legs gave way. She fell heavily on something. It felt warm and furry and the feel of it repelled her. What was it? An animal? The Chupacabra itself? She squirmed away until she could feel the hard ground beneath her again and then lay still. Total exhaustion overcame her. Instead of leaping to her feet, she lay waiting for the Chupacabra to strike; she could smell him in the air. Vanessa began to shiver uncontrollably.

CHAPTER 1

The Chupacabra is a mysterious creature that has killed thousands of farm animals in Mexico and other Central and South American countries. The strange thing is that it kills its prey by draining their blood. As goats were the first reported victims, this deadly cryptid has been called *el Chupacabra*, which is Spanish for "the goat sucker."

He looked like an army general—an immaculate green uniform with brass buttons, a stiff peaked hat, and a gun in a highly polished holster at his hip.

Vanessa and Nikki gave him their best smiles. But even that wasn't enough to change his expression. He stared sullenly at them.

"*Pasaporte*," he said abruptly. When he continued in a stream of Spanish the girls looked at each other helplessly.

"*Lo siento*, sorry," Vanessa said as they handed him their passports. She hoped that an apology in Spanish might soften him up.

No joy. He took a long time examining their passports and then looked up doubtfully. The girls squeezed each other's hands and hoped he wouldn't ask them any more questions in Spanish. Finally he stamped the passports with a vigor that seemed quite over-the-top and, with a wave of his hand, dismissed them.

They bolted through to the baggage hall and found the carousel. While they waited for their bags they laughed about "the general." It had been funny but a bit scary too.

"OK, customs now. Hopefully we won't get arrested or—"

"Don't even think it, Vanessa!" Nikki burst out. She wasn't used to traveling as Vanessa was.

It was a huge relief when they finally made it to the arrivals hall where Nikki's aunt and uncle were supposed to be meeting them. Unfortunately it was very crowded; way too crowded. The girls stopped and scanned the sea of faces.

"Wow, I know that Mexico City has over twenty million people, but I didn't think they would all be at the airport to meet us," Vanessa tried to joke. "I wonder . . ."

But the look on her friend's face stopped her. Nikki was very worried now—she looked close to tears.

"We'll find them, Nikki, or they will find us. Either way we'll be fine," Vanessa reassured her.

The words were no sooner out of Vanessa's mouth than she spotted them. She elbowed Nikki and pointed, her finger trembling in excitement.

"Look, over there. Isn't that your Uncle Joseph? I think I recognize him from the photograph you have. He's looking around, but he hasn't seen us yet. Go on, wave, see if he waves back." Vanessa hesitated. "But . . . is that . . . could that really be your aunt?"

The woman beside Joseph was staring into the distance. She looked cool and detached, like a film star from an old movie. She was dark-skinned with inky black hair knotted high on her head. She was tall and slim, with the tiniest waist Vanessa had ever seen. But most striking was the way she was dressed: a fitted top with jewels sewn into the neckline and layers of colorful skirts right down to the ground!

"I don't know." Nikki shrugged. "Never met her before. Her name's Frida, and she's Mexican; that's all I know."

"She looks as if she's going to get out her castanets and dance across the terminal," Vanessa said, craning her neck to see if there was anyone else waiting for them. "No sign of your cousins, though."

Nikki's cousins were around their own age, a girl of thirteen and a boy of fifteen. Vanessa hoped desperately that they would be OK. She and Nikki were going to be spending four weeks with them on their ranch, after all. At first glance Frida certainly looked a bit strange. But at least Joseph was reassuringly normal. Stocky, with a bit of a belly. A real red-faced Irish farmer.

Nikki gave a hesitant wave, and when the man's face lit up and he hurried toward them, they knew they had hit the jackpot.

"Actually, I'm more interested in that other man

standing beside them. The one who looks like he's just been to band practice," said Nikki.

Vanessa giggled. Her friend was herself again. The porter did look striking in his bright-red uniform with gold buttons and black trim.

"Posh or what? They certainly like their uniforms over here," Vanessa muttered as they walked over to meet Nikki's aunt and uncle.

Frida said nothing when Joseph introduced her to the girls, just gave a ghost of a smile. Maybe she didn't speak much English, and their Spanish certainly needed work. That was one of the reasons Vanessa's father had allowed her to make this trip.

The porter took the girls' wheelie bags and led the way out of the terminal building and into a blast of Mexican heat and noise. Horns were honking, people shouting, trolleys trundling and children crying all around them. Wow, they had really arrived!

Vanessa found the sun blinding and dived into her bag for her sunglasses. When she looked up again, Nikki had moved a few steps ahead and appeared to be talking to Frida. She couldn't make out what they were saying. Were they speaking English or Spanish?

Vanessa hung back a little more—she was tired and it was nice to have a moment to herself. The airport had been stressful, but it was great to be here. She loved the intense sunshine, the feel of the heat on her skin, but she was definitely feeling a bit lightheaded too.

Vanessa's eye was caught by a young woman in jeans and a white shirt walking slowly toward her.

She looked quite ordinary at first, but then Vanessa noticed something strange. No, she wasn't walking, exactly; she was gliding, floating along a couple of inches above the ground. Vanessa blinked. The heat must really be getting to her, she thought. She was about to call out to Nikki but her voice caught in her throat. OK, the woman was not just floating now, she was also wearing . . . was it a coat of feathers? And a mask, maybe—something with a beak, anyway. What on earth was going on?

Vanessa ran forward and grabbed Nikki by the elbow. Nikki and Frida both looked around.

"What's wrong?" Nikki asked. "You look like you've seen a ghost."

"Look!" said Vanessa, pointing. But the bird woman had disappeared. "I could have sworn I saw . . . a giant bird. Or . . . I mean, maybe a woman dressed as a bird."

Nikki laughed. "Oh, Vanessa! That imagination of yours."

Friends often told her that she was fanciful. "Full of notions," her father called it. But Vanessa knew better. Sometimes she really did see things that other people couldn't.

"No, no, I really did . . ."

Frida said nothing but gave Vanessa a long, cool look from under her heavy black eyebrows.

"It was probably someone in fancy dress," said Nikki soothingly. "Maybe there's a festival on. It is Mexico, you know."

Yes, it was Mexico, and it was a long way from Dublin. A small window of anxiety opened up in Vanessa, but she said nothing.

"Come on, girls," called Joseph in his Galway accent. "The limo's waiting."

And it really was a limousine—long, black, and sleek, with a chauffeur in another uniform and a peaked cap. Nikki thought it looked beautiful, but it reminded Vanessa of a funeral car. She gave a little shudder as she climbed in.

CHAPTER 2

Where Chupacabra attacks have happened, the authorities have tried to attribute the killings to known predators such as dogs, foxes, hyenas, or coyotes. But in most cases there have been puncture wounds in the necks of the animals through which the blood has been drained, and this has never been explained satisfactorily.

The road they took from the airport was extremely busy. Trucks spilled over with fruits and vegetables, and flatbed trucks were piled high with old fridges and TVs. Most of the cars were so old that Vanessa was amazed they could move at all.

"Look at that one, Nikki," she said, pointing to a car with no windscreen. "Its hood is tied down with string."

"There's a swanky car, though," said Nikki. "It's got tinted windows."

"Drug dealer," said Joseph. "Or maybe a politician. Either way, it'll be bulletproof."

Vanessa and Nikki exchanged glances. Bulletproof!

"Coke cheap—almost free!" Vanessa heard someone shout when they stopped at a traffic light. It was a boy, holding bottles up to the car windows as he strolled between the cars. He looked about ten, the same age as her younger brother, Ronan, and yet there he was, out on the street dodging traffic and trying to earn some money.

Most of the houses they passed were only half built, with rooms open to the streets. The girls pointed things out to each other: an old man sitting in an armchair, strumming his guitar, in the middle of the pavement; a toddler playing with pots and pans on his own, too close to the road. It was all so strange and very different from Ireland.

"How much longer to the ranch?" Vanessa asked Nikki as they drove along.

"Another three hours," Joseph chipped in.

Three hours! It had been a very long day already.

"Have a sleep, maybe," Joseph suggested.

It was all too exciting to sleep, though. Nikki plugged her earphones into her iPod and Vanessa pulled a folder out of her backpack.

"You're not going to study, are you?" Nikki asked.

"You know me. I just want to brush up on my Spanish verbs," Vanessa joked and then laughed at the expression on Nikki's face.

Nikki grabbed the folder and read the heading.

"*El Chupacabra*. Oh, so it is Spanish after all. What does it mean?"

"It roughly translates into English as 'the goat-sucker,'" Vanessa said with great emphasis on the words.

"Eeuugh!" said Nikki. "That's disgusting. What on earth are you reading?"

"Oh, cryptozoology," said Vanessa casually.

"What?"

"It's the study of cryptids . . . kind of like weird animals. The Loch Ness monster is one. Remember, my mum was always interested in them."

"Oh, sorry," said Nikki. "Your mum . . ."

"It's OK," said Vanessa. "I like to remember her. This is one of her folders that I found in the attic. It's about a Mexican cryptid—the Chupacabra. It kills its prey by . . ."

"On second thought," Nikki said quickly, "I don't really want to know, thanks, Vanessa."

CHAPTER 3

There have been many eyewitness accounts of the Chupacabra. While they vary in detail, most describe a creature with four legs. It can walk upright or jump on two legs when it chooses. It is fast and agile and prowls at night.

The entrance to the ranch was marked by an impressive set of gates. Grand enough to lead to a French chateau rather than just a farm, Vanessa thought. The tops of the gates were elegantly arched and the word *Martinez* was inset in wrought iron.

"What does Martinez mean?" asked Vanessa.

"I'm Frida Martinez." It was the first time she had spoken to Vanessa. Her voice was throaty and she was very abrupt.

Vanessa started. "Oh, I see," she mumbled.

"My grandfather came here over one hundred years ago from Barcelona. This is the biggest ranch in the area. Six thousand acres."

The odd thing about the entrance was that the gates stood alone. There were no railings or fences running from them, no barbed wire as there would be on an Irish farm, only the huge gates standing in glorious isolation.

The car swung through the gates and Vanessa and Nikki squeezed each other's hands in anticipation. A cloud of red dust rose up around them as the tires hit a pothole and spun free.

Tall trees lined the driveway for the first few hundred feet, but they soon dwindled out, and it became more of a dirt track than a drive. Around them the flat open fields stretched into the distance, dotted with cacti and small trees with gnarled trunks.

At last a low, sprawling stone house came into view, shimmering in the afternoon heat. It was old and very beautiful, with huge stone pillars and a veranda.

Vanessa got out of the car, trying to pack up her bag at the same time. She was startled when a pack of dogs of all shapes and sizes appeared from behind the house and ran toward them, barking noisily.

There were two spaniels with bloodshot eyes, a huge Alsatian, and two small terriers with ridiculously short legs. But Vanessa's eye was caught by a weird-looking dog that was standing apart from the pack. He was black and entirely hairless. This one stood absolutely immobile, looking directly at Vanessa, his ears pricked. They were large triangular ears, more like a bat's ears than a dog's, and far too big for his small head. His body was muscular, and his broad shoulders were tensed like a boxer's.

Vanessa was just about to say something to Nikki about the dog when a girl emerged from the house, shouting at the dogs in Spanish.

"Vanessa, that's my cousin, Carmen!" said Nikki.

"I've seen a photo of her. Isn't she pretty?"

Carmen's jet-black hair was cut in a straight fringe and was tied in two long plaits. Her clothes looked expensive: a white linen dress and leather sandals. She was way too dressed up for a dusty ranch, Vanessa thought.

At the sound of Carmen's voice, most of the dogs had dropped to the ground and rolled onto their backs for a tummy rub. It was hard not to be impressed. The hairless dog remained standing, however, still as a garden statue, watching Vanessa.

"You're very welcome, Nikki and Vanessa," Carmen said in perfect English, putting out her hand like an adult.

At least she was being friendly. Where was the brother, though? Vanessa wondered. Armado, Nikki had said he was called. She liked the name.

"It's four o'clock," Joseph said as they entered the house. "Siesta time."

"I'll take you to your bedrooms and then to the kitchen for some hibiscus water if you like," Carmen offered.

Bedrooms? That was disappointing. They had hoped they would be sharing.

The first room was dark and cool, but when Carmen opened the shutters, the sunshine streamed in and Vanessa could see horses grazing in the fields outside.

"The other bedroom is just next door," Carmen said, opening double doors that led outside to a terrace with a small table and chairs. Farther along, an identical set of double doors opened into the next bedroom. At least they were right beside each other.

"My bedroom is just there." Carmen pointed to another door farther down along the terrace. "I'll show you around the house later, and my brother Mado will show you the ranch."

Vanessa grinned at Nikki. Mexico was great, and she really liked what she had seen of the ranch so far. Aunt Frida was not exactly friendly, but Carmen seemed perfectly nice. Hopefully Armado would be all right too. She surprised herself by letting out a sigh of relief.

"Tired?" Carmen asked her.

"Beyond tiredness, I think," Vanessa replied, "and parched."

Vanessa and Nikki followed Carmen through a warren of corridors.

"I'll take you to the kitchen for a drink and to meet Izel. She's our cook," Carmen said over her shoulder.

Vanessa raised her eyebrows. Imagine having your own cook! It was a different world.

CHAPTER 4

On 9 May 1996 at 2:00 A.M. in Sinaloa, Mexico, the Espinoza family saw the Chupacabra. It was about 3 to 4 feet high with scaly skin, clawed hands, red eyes, and a row of spines from the skullcap down the back. Mr. Espinoza said that "it mumbled and gestured." Two of the children said it "smelled like a wet dog."

In the end Vanessa was too excited to sleep that afternoon. She got up from her bed and took out her charcoals and sketch pad. She tried to draw what she imagined the Chupacabra looked like—the ridgy spine, the claws, the raw gums and pointed teeth.

After a couple of attempts she abandoned it and sketched the Loch Ness monster instead. Nessie was a pleasure to draw, and the backs of Vanessa's copybooks in school were filled with doodles of her.

She called to mind the graceful curve of Nessie's head and her trusting, seal-like eyes. It would be hard to make a malformed, ugly dog with blood-sucking tendencies look cute.

Vanessa opened her wallet and took out a small picture of her mum. The right-hand corner was curled from being held so often, and there was a tiny tear on the bottom that she needed to repair sometime. The photo had been taken years before her mother got sick. Vanessa missed her so much.

She smiled sadly at the picture and whispered, "Oh, Mum, I wish you were here. You probably wouldn't like Frida either. She is unfriendly and cold and ... and ..."

Vanessa stopped, realizing that she could not quite put her feelings into words. There was something more than that wrong with Frida. But what exactly was it?

A gong sounded in the distance. A gong? Could

it be for dinner? She checked her watch. It was nine o'clock, much later than she had imagined. Her dad had been right when he said that they ate at funny times in Mexico. She'd still have time to wash her hands and face, surely, but probably not to change her clothes.

Everyone was sitting at a huge table when she finally arrived in the dining room. Everyone including an amazing-looking boy, a bit older than she was, she guessed. This had to be Armado.

He said very little when Joseph introduced them. Vanessa hoped she could sit beside Nikki, but Carmen was on one side of her and Frida on the other. The only space left was beside Armado.

The dining table looked very formal, set with white china and silver cutlery. On every plate a starched white napkin was curled neatly inside a napkin holder. Vanessa thought it looked very elegant—she certainly couldn't imagine her brothers at this table. No muddy tracksuits and T-shirts here. Everyone in the Martinez family had changed for dinner. Vanessa looked down at her own clothes, tired and crumpled from the journey. At least Nikki looked just as bad as she did. Surely they didn't do this every night?

They all bowed their heads while Frida said grace in Spanish. The four-course dinner was served by a young girl who kept her eyes averted no matter how friendly Vanessa tried to be.

Silently they ate parcels of deep fried something-or-other on mounds of salad leaves. Vanessa nibbled at the edge of the parcel hoping that it wouldn't be too spicy. Her dad had warned her that they used chilies in every dish in Mexico. *Right again, Dad.*

"This is a local dish, *enchiladas mineras*," Frida announced suddenly. "The next course will be Aztec soup, followed by sweet roasted chicken stuffed with figs and a dessert of hibiscus flower ice cream."

It was like being in a restaurant where the chef comes around to explain the dishes. But Vanessa knew that Frida hadn't been slaving in the kitchen all afternoon. They had met Izel, the cook, earlier, and she had been busy preparing dinner—no sign of Frida then.

"Don't forget, Armado, the engineers are coming tomorrow to discuss the new well," Joseph was saying to his son. "We have a water shortage on the ranch," he explained to the girls.

"I suppose it doesn't rain here very often," said Vanessa. "It's always raining in Ireland."

"Oh, but it does. We have two seasons in Mexico: the dry and the wet," Armado explained. He had a lovely accent. "We get huge rainstorms that fill the rivers and reservoirs, but in the last few years there hasn't been enough rain. Well, not on this ranch anyhow."

"It's the curse," Carmen muttered darkly.

Frida shot her daughter a look that silenced her. Vanessa was dying to ask what Carmen meant.

Did she mean a real curse, like witchcraft?

"Do you ride?" Armado suddenly asked Vanessa. She gave a small jump in her chair. A blush started at her neck and rose up her face. She really hated that.

"No, but I'd love to learn."

Frida's fork stopped midair, and she stared rudely. What on earth was wrong with her now?

"Remember, the girls will be busy in the afternoons with their chores, Armado," Frida said stiffly. "You will be part of the family while you are here, Vanessa and Nikki," Frida explained, "and you will do chores in the afternoons, like Carmen."

Chores? Vanessa shot a look at Armado. How about him, did he do chores too? Armado met her gaze evenly and smiled. Did he know what she was thinking?

"After your chores I would suggest that you take a siesta, but then your time is your own, as long as you do not interfere with the running of the ranch."

What on earth did that mean, interfere with the running of the ranch? Vanessa felt a knot twisting in the pit of her stomach. She put her knife and fork down. She couldn't eat another morsel.

"In the evenings, then," Armado suggested. "We can go riding when it's cooler."

"Next week I will begin your Spanish lessons," Frida went on, ignoring Armado. "For an hour in the morning, immediately after breakfast."

Vanessa was appalled. Spanish classes with Frosty Frida followed by chores and a siesta! This was not how it was meant to be. They were supposed to be having an amazing adventure in Mexico, riding horses and running wild for the summer.

Miserably, Vanessa stared at her plate, and tears pricked at the corners of her eyes. She suddenly felt very homesick. She missed her dad and her brothers. She was almost sorry she'd come to this weird place. She didn't dare to lift her eyes to look at Nikki; she was too embarrassed at the thought of crying in front of Frida and Armado.

CHAPTER 5

The puncture wounds made by the Chupacabra are small, about a quarter of an inch in size, but very deep, going completely through the layers of muscle tissue.

Vanessa didn't sleep well that night. At first she left a window open to the terrace to try and dilute the still, hot air in her room, but the screech of unknown animals in the night and the constant buzz of insects soon changed her mind. She didn't fall into a deep sleep until about four o'clock and was exhausted when she woke to the sound of a knock on her bedroom door.

"Breakfast is at eight in the courtyard, Vanessa." Carmen kissed her on both cheeks and then stared shyly at her. "You look more tired than yesterday. It is the jet lag, I believe."

Vanessa dressed quickly and found her way to the flower-filled courtyard.

Frida appeared wearing a long silk robe and gold flip-flops. She drank her espresso silently while the three girls chatted. Afterwards she showed them into a huge sitting room. Large brass fans circulated slowly in the ceiling, and the polished wooden floorboards gleamed. The walls were filled with framed photographs, most of them very old-looking. The enormous fireplace was flanked by two full-sized carved wooden dogs.

"Oh, look!" cried Nikki, her eyes on the dogs. "Aren't they lovely? So lifelike."

Frida stroked one of their heads, and Vanessa was surprised by the look of affection on her face.

"Marco and Polo were my grandfather's hunting dogs. They used to sit at his feet every evening when he was reading."

Frida turned to the other dog and stroked its head in turn.

"When they died he carved these to keep him company."

"Carved them himself?" asked Vanessa, impressed.

"Oh, yes, he was an art student in Spain before he came here. My grandmother also. She died not long after they arrived in Mexico."

For a split second Vanessa found herself looking around the room in case there was a wooden replica of Frida's grandmother on display too. Instead her eyes were caught by glass-fronted cabinets that were filled with guns and knives.

"Wow, an old fashioned blunderbuss," she said. She suppressed a smile when she caught Frida's frozen expression of surprise. No doubt only boys were supposed to know such things. She was dying to open the doors and take the antique weapons out, but she didn't dare.

"Is this you, Frida?" Vanessa asked instead, looking at a photograph of a young girl. She was smiling up at an older woman who was staring straight at the camera.

For a moment Vanessa thought that Frida wasn't

going to answer her. Maybe it was rude to have called her Frida. Should she have said Señora Martinez?

"Yes, that is me," Frida finally answered.

"And that's your mother, I guess. You look so much like her." Vanessa turned and smiled, but Frida bristled visibly and then turned away.

Confused by Frida's reaction, Vanessa turned back quickly to look at the other photos. She had meant it as a compliment. She loved it when people said she was like her own mother.

"And now embroidery, please," Frida said.

Startled out of her own thoughts, Vanessa saw Frida holding a piece of white linen in one hand and a needle and thread in the other. So this was what she meant by chores! Vanessa had hoped she would be working with the animals, milking cows, mucking out stables. But embroidery? She hoped it would be easy to do. She had never held a needle before, never mind done intricate designs.

Vanessa flopped down on the sofa beside Nikki and dug her elbow gently into her friend's ribs. Nikki looked at her, and Vanessa grinned.

"How long do you reckon we'll have to do this for?" Vanessa said softly.

"Two hours," Frida answered coldly. "It is part of a community project here. We sell the tablecloths and napkins to tourists and raise funds for the orphanage in Guanajuato."

Vanessa stared down at the cloth. There was a leaf pattern outlined around the edges. They wouldn't be able to sell her effort for much, that was for sure.

"Just use the green thread and follow the outline," Carmen explained. "It is not that hard, really."

Vanessa secretly rolled her eyes and stabbed her needle into the cloth.

Frida left the room, and Vanessa gave a sigh of relief.

She pulled the thread through. Not too bad, she thought, jabbing the needle in again—right into her middle finger. A bead of bright red blood bloomed on her knuckle. She watched as the blood spread to stain the white linen.

She swore, shouted, outraged, and threw the cloth down.

Carmen and Nikki stared at each other and then collapsed laughing.

It was not a great start. Vanessa would willingly give every last peso she had to the orphanage rather than spend the morning sitting here sewing politely and bleeding all over her efforts.

It was their second day on the ranch, and except for going outside on the veranda to play with the dogs, she had seen nothing of it yet, she thought miserably. Was this going to be their daily chore? It was gruesome, and she didn't think she could last a month at it.

Then an idea occurred to her. What if she volunteered to work at something different?

"Carmen, what does Armado do in the line of chores?" she asked. "I know my brothers are pretty lazy around the house," she added in an attempt to make her question sound casual.

"During the holidays he works all day on the ranch from six in the morning. Papa has only four other ranch hands to work the entire estate. Mado works very hard."

Carmen spoke proudly. She clearly adored her older brother.

A small kernel of envy lodged itself in Vanessa's throat, and she smiled wistfully back. It didn't sound as if she would be allowed to work out of doors anyway. That was boys' work, obviously. Maybe she could volunteer to help in the kitchen, though? Izel, the cook, had seemed nice.

Vanessa looked out the window and caught sight of Armado cantering across the field on a beautiful black horse, lasso in hand, looking just like a real Mexican cowboy. It was all very disheartening.

"Speak of the devil!" Vanessa said out loud.

Carmen's head shot up. "Don't say that," she gasped.

Vanessa laughed. But when she saw the look of terror on Carmen's face she stopped immediately.

"Bad word," Carmen said.

"I'm so sorry, Carmen, it's just a saying in English," explained Vanessa. "It's nothing to do with the actual devil. Honestly. I happened to see Armado as we were speaking about him, that's all."

Carmen stared at Vanessa, her eyes wide. She still looked worried.

"*Esta bien*, Carmen?" Nikki touched her cousin's arm gently.

"It is just that *Rancho del Diablo* is what the locals sometimes call this place. Devil Ranch."

"Why on earth . . . ?" asked Vanessa.

"I am not sure. I think it is something to do with

animals that go missing or get killed on this ranch. They say it is cursed."

"Is that the curse that you were talking about at dinner last night?" Vanessa asked.

Carmen suddenly clammed up.

"No, no, it is nothing. I should not speak of it."

"But why is it cursed?" persisted Vanessa. Carmen said nothing.

"Animals die all the time on a ranch, don't they?" Vanessa said, ignoring Nikki's warning frown. It was obvious that Carmen was uncomfortable talking about it.

Carmen's reply was almost inaudible: "Not this way."

CHAPTER 6

The Nahua people in Mexico date back to pre-Columbian times and are considered the direct descendants of the Aztecs. They live mostly in central Mexico, and it is estimated that 1.4 million people speak the language Nahuatl. They are a highly spiritual people and have strong belief in the forces of good and evil. *Izel* is a Nahuatl name meaning "unique."

Vanessa volunteered for kitchen duties. Anything was better than embroidery. Frida had not been too pleased about it, but she could hardly argue with a guest who was prepared to help out with the cooking, so she took Vanessa to the kitchen and introduced her to Izel as the new kitchen assistant. Izel was delighted with the idea. Her black eyes shone warmly, and she threw her arms around Vanessa, hugging her like a long-lost daughter. Vanessa smiled to herself. She liked this woman already.

The Martinezes' cook was the most remarkable shape. At five-foot nothing, she had broad shoulders, thick calves, a shelf-like chest and a simply enormous waist.

While Frida and Izel chatted away in Spanish, their hands clasped together and heads bent over like penguins, Vanessa was amazed to hear Frida laugh. Maybe she was only cold to Vanessa because she didn't know her. She clearly adored Izel.

Not wanting to appear to be listening, Vanessa looked around the kitchen. It was a world away from their cramped kitchen at home—about four times the size and flooded with light from the large windows to the front.

The countertop was crammed with ceramic bowls piled with fruits and vegetables that Vanessa didn't recognize. On a long shelf above the counter there were dozens of glass jars filled with dried herbs. They had white labels with spidery handwriting on them— Izel's writing, Vanessa guessed. The jars looked more like something out of an old-fashioned pharmacy than a kitchen. Over the enormous black stove copper pots hung from brass hooks on wooden racks and ranged in size from milk pan to army issue.

Frida left without another glance at Vanessa, and Izel stood alone—a queen in her kitchen kingdom, her face beaming.

"Vanessa, I like you wash the hands with the soap, and we start."

Vanessa was amused by the contrast of her clear, hard voice compared to her soft and rounded appearance.

"*De prisa*, hurry, we have much to do."

Izel was standing by an enormous sink, holding up the soap. She turned on the water.

"I make it myself. It is lemon and wild ginger."

"Sounds like you should eat it rather than wash with it."

Izel chuckled, her chest wobbling. This was going to be much more fun than Vanessa had expected.

Soon Vanessa had learned how to chop onions

very finely using a razor-sharp knife. One slip and her finger would be off, though. This was followed by a demonstration on how to skin tomatoes by dropping them in boiling water. Things were going well.

The telephone rang in the hall, and Izel disappeared to answer it. Vanessa continued to slice mangos and eyed the result with pleasure. She was getting good at this—not the mess of pulp she ended up with the first time she tried.

Izel was still on the phone, and through the open door Vanessa could hear her voice rising and falling but she couldn't understand the words. Occasionally she shouted something like "galote," and Vanessa wondered if that was the person's name. She finished slicing the mangos and went to the sink to wash the knife and plate she had been using.

Vanessa stared out the kitchen window at the fields, which stretched out for miles. Tomorrow evening they would be going on their first horse-riding lesson with Armado. Frida had finally given in.

Suddenly a face appeared at the window and gave her the fright of her life. It was a man's face, his nose pressed against the glass. His eyes locked onto hers, dull and impassive, and the vacant look in them scared Vanessa. He had long, greasy hair and baggy, lined skin under his eyes. Slowly his cruel, thin lips parted in a sneer, revealing large gaps and uneven teeth in decaying gums. Vanessa gave a small scream and grabbed the knife from the sink.

She turned quickly when she heard Izel's loud shout behind her. Izel must have seen the face as well, because she was rabbiting on in some unintelligible language and throwing her hands up. The only word Vanessa could make out seemed to be "sholo," whatever that meant.

Bewildered, Vanessa accidentally knocked a plate off the drainer, and it smashed into a thousand pieces on the tile floor. Now the hairless dog she had seen when she first arrived at the ranch had appeared out of nowhere and was barking at Vanessa's feet.

It was all too much for her. Her heart racing, she hopped up onto the kitchen counter, still clutching the knife in her hands and staring down at the dog.

When their eyes met, the dog stopped barking as suddenly as he had started. His bat-like ears stood upright on his strange, torpedo-shaped head. What on earth had gotten into the dog? Had she stood on his paw?

Next thing, she saw Izel moving quickly across the kitchen as if powered by the stream of her words, with her arms flapping wildly. Finally Vanessa caught some Spanish words that she understood.

"*Perro malo, perro malo!*" Bad dog. Phew, it was only the dog Izel was shouting at and not her. Suddenly remembering the man at the window, Vanessa glanced behind her again, but the face had gone. Maybe Izel hadn't seen the man after all, and it was the dog she was upset about.

She certainly looked cross. She stood with her hands on her hips talking down to the animal, stopping occasionally as if she expected him to answer back. Instead, the dog turned and walked out the kitchen door and past Izel without a second glance.

"That dog knows he is not allowed in my kitchen," Izel said indignantly. Vanessa, still clueless as to what exactly was going on, smiled despite herself.

"He has never come into my kitchen before. I do not know what has got into him. It is you he came to see, I think." She looked at Vanessa, who was still up on the counter with the knife in her hand.

Tilting her head slightly to one side Izel added

more calmly, "But you do not need to protect yourself from Sholo."

"Sholo?" asked Vanessa, climbing down off the counter. "Is that the dog?"

"Yes. It's the make of dog he is."

"Oh, the breed, you mean? How do you spell it?"

"X-o-l-o. It is said as Sholo. It is the sacred dog of the Aztecs but Xolo is also this one's name."

Vanessa's mind reeled as she tried to take in the words.

Izel took Vanessa's hand and eased the knife out of it gently.

"Xolo would never hurt you—not you. No, he will protect you."

Vanessa didn't know what to say to that, so she started to pick up the pieces of the broken plate.

"Sorry, Izel, about the plate. I got a fright when the dog barked. I didn't see him come in."

She didn't want to mention the face at the window. Nikki might say it was another of her notions, and maybe Izel wouldn't believe her either. But she wondered if the dog had seen the face at the window too. Maybe that was why he had barked. Was he really trying to protect her? And from whom?

Izel took a few avocados from the pile in front of her and handed Vanessa another knife.

"That was my son on the phone," she said after a moment.

"Is his name Galote or Gwaylotay or something like that?" asked Vanessa, remembering the word she'd overheard.

Izel threw back her head on her thick neck and roared with laughter.

"No, no, *chica*, it's Miguel," she said, her voice warm with affection. "*Guajolote* means turkey in my language." She began to chuckle again. "I call him that when he is being a silly boy."

"In Spanish, you mean?"

"No, in Nahuatl. That is my language. We are the Nahua people."

Izel lifted her many chins, her voice filled with pride.

"Does he work on the ranch?" Vanessa asked. "Your son, I mean."

"No, he is in the United States. He is studying there. What about you? What kind of work you like to do when you are older?"

"I want to be a cryptozoologist," Vanessa said.

This might be a bit difficult to explain, she thought. "It's a sort of scientist, really. Like my mum was."

"Science is good. You must be a clever girl. I think you are very good at exams the way Frida was at school."

No sooner had she said the words than the door to the kitchen swung open, and Frida stood taking in the scene. She seemed to have a remarkable sense of timing; it was really quite freaky.

"How are you getting along, Vanessa?" Frida said coolly. "Do you still prefer cooking to embroidery?"

CHAPTER 7

Belief in magic and sorcery is still strong in rural Mexico, particularly among the Nahua people. "Airs" are associated with the dead—they hang around where someone has died. Airs have been described as being like the biting wind that sweeps across the land just before a thunderstorm. Some airs can be evil and dangerous.

Vanessa had been worried about embarrassing herself at her first riding lesson. But from the moment she sat across Amigo's solid back with her feet in the stirrups, she felt comfortable. More than comfortable—it felt natural.

Before long she was trotting and then cantering. But when she started to gallop, Armado shouted at her to slow down.

"It's your first lesson!" he called, riding up beside her. "You have to slow down."

"But it's wonderful!" she cried and galloped away from him again.

She couldn't resist shouting out with delight, her long hair streaming behind her and her cheeks flushed with excitement.

There was a fallen tree ahead. She'd love to try jumping over that, but Armado would be furious with her. Maybe next time.

"Are you sure you have never ridden before, Vanessa?" Armado had come alongside her again. "You are amazing!"

Vanessa smiled at him and mentally hugged that little snippet of praise to herself.

It was a pity that Nikki had backed out of the lesson at the last minute. When she saw the size of her horse and the way he had stamped and snorted while he was being saddled up, Nikki had finally admitted to being very nervous and not at all eager to learn to ride.

"I'll take one of the bikes out when we go exploring," Nikki had insisted. "That will suit me just fine."

Both Armado and Vanessa had done their best to persuade her; she stood sweet but firm.

About an hour after they had set out Vanessa felt a cold wind pick up, and within minutes it had grown darker. She looked up and saw thick gray clouds massing overhead. She shivered, chilled suddenly. How could the weather change so quickly? And then the heavens opened, and it started to rain. It came down in huge, fat drops like nothing she'd ever experienced before. Her vision became blurred as the rainwater streamed down her face. It felt exactly like her morning shower, especially as the rain was lukewarm, not cold as in Ireland.

Vanessa looked around for Armado as cracks of thunder loud enough to shake the ground sounded overhead. Not so pleasant anymore.

But Armado had his head back, his face tilted skyward. He shouted something which at first Vanessa couldn't hear over the noise of the rain and thunder. He was clearly enjoying it.

"It's wonderful to feel the rain at last," he yelled louder this time. "But we need to get the horses out of the storm. I know a place. Follow me."

Armado's horse, Zoro, reared and snorted and was distressed by the thunder, but Vanessa's horse, Amigo, remained surprisingly calm.

Armado led Vanessa to a derelict stone house. Its corrugated iron roof had grass growing on it and tree branches sticking out through it. It didn't look up to much, but Vanessa could see that there was a sheltered space at the front for the horses.

Armado tied the reins of both horses to a hook on the wall. Although they were under cover now, Zoro was getting more nervous with each thunder-crack. Vanessa hated to see his distress and stood beside him, stroking his neck and making low guttural sounds in her throat that seemed to calm him.

Armado stared at her in open admiration.

"You're just like Cesar," he said.

"Who?"

"He's one of the ranch hands. All he has to do is whisper something and the horses understand him. I've tried to copy the sounds, but it doesn't work for me. How did you learn to do that?"

"I didn't. I just made what I thought were soothing noises. It's not like I can talk to the animals."

"Well, Xolo definitely understands you. He's like a guard dog around you now." Armado said it lightly, but Vanessa was struck by his words. Should she tell him about Xolo barking in the kitchen yesterday? Or that this morning she had found the dog outside her bedroom on the terrace? He had been sitting like a statue looking out across the fields, his muscular haunches much more visible than a normal dog's because he was hairless. He certainly didn't behave like a typical pet, but she did not find him threatening either.

Then another thought struck her, and she tried to sneak a look at Armado's face to see his expression. Maybe Izel had told Armado how Vanessa had grabbed the knife and jumped up on the counter yesterday. Maybe he was teasing her.

She ran her hand along the length of Amigo's neck, feeling the smooth hair and his soft warm mouth against her arm as he nuzzled her. Animals were so much easier to understand.

"The storm doesn't seem to bother Amigo," she said.

"Yes, he is steady."

"Good boy. I suppose you are used to this weather, aren't you?" Vanessa said, stroking the horse's neck.

"No, that's not the reason. He is actually deaf," Armado said with a huge grin. "Thunder doesn't bother him."

Vanessa stared at him, unsure for a moment whether he was joking or not.

"It is true. But stand in front of him and he can lip-read very well."

Now he was joking. Vanessa laughed and punched him on the shoulder, with her middle knuckle slightly raised for extra effect the way she did to Luke and Ronan.

Armado gave a mock yelp and turned away. Vanessa suddenly felt a bit foolish. She sensed that Carmen would never have punched her beloved brother like that. And a guest certainly shouldn't. Oh dear.

CHAPTER 8

A shaman is an individual who has the power to heal and protect people in his or her community. The ability comes directly from supernatural beings through dreams, visions, or spirit possession, all of which happen during shamanistic ceremonies. Stones that have a hole through the middle of them are used in these ceremonies and are called sacred stones; the hole is the doorway to the spirit world. The use of feathers is particularly important, as birds are seen as the messengers of the spirits.

Vanessa twisted her hair between her fingers and

squeezed the water out of it.

"No need to have showered today," she said. "Let's go inside."

Armado hesitated for a moment.

"OK," he said. "I would quite like to show you something anyway."

There was a narrow hallway in the house, which was damp and depressing. Four small, grim rooms led off it. The rain hammered relentlessly on the metal roof, and the drumming sound reminded Vanessa of the caravan holidays they used to have in Wexford when she was young. But there was a difference here: the rain was coming through the roof and was trickling down the inside walls.

"It rains inside this house," Armado said, "but the odd thing is, there is one room that is always dry. I don't know how."

"Well," said Vanessa, "maybe it's got a good bit of roof over it."

"No, from the outside it looks just as bad as the rest. It's strange."

Vanessa stepped into the dry room and looked around. There were stones and feathers scattered around as if a chicken had been plucked recently.

At first all she felt was the extreme cold, and then came the nasty smell. She glanced sideways at Armado, but he showed no reaction. He picked up two chairs that were lying on their sides beside a battered little table that had also been turned over and lay stranded like a cockroach on its back. Armado made a motion for her to sit.

As Vanessa lowered herself onto a chair, a strange fluttering sensation began in her stomach. She put her hands on the table to steady herself. The fluttering became a constriction in her gut, which crept up to her heart and throat, paralyzing her. Then came a violent assault: a rush of emotions twisting inside her like a tornado that was impossible to describe. She clutched the edges of the table in terror, her knuckles white, her arms shaking.

"Vanessa, Vanessa, what is the matter?"

Armado's face was suddenly close to hers, but she turned away and found herself looking into another face—thin, dark, with hawk-like eyes. The image broke up like a glass puzzle shattering in the air, the pieces slipping in and out as if from another time and place—red glowing eyes, a gaping mouth, bloody fangs, a bird's beak, a string of feathers around a neck.

All her senses felt exposed—the light too bright, the roaring noise too loud, the stench too foul.

Vanessa pushed violently back with her feet and the chair screeched loudly on the tiled floor. She felt a hand grab her upper arm, and she fought it off desperately. Her tongue was thick and dry as it moved along the back of her teeth, but she couldn't speak. Her eyes grew so hot that they burned in their sockets. Then she passed out.

When Vanessa opened her eyes, Armado was leaning over her, his face so close that she could feel his breath. He looked anxious. Even in her confusion she noticed how dark his eyes were, how long his eyelashes.

It took her a few moments to realize that she was lying on the floor. Armado pulled back as she made an effort to get up.

Gingerly she sat upright and gazed around the room. With some effort her eyes focused on the chair where she had been sitting. It was on its side again. The table, too, was upturned.

There was little else in the room—a rusting rake against a wall and a wooden barrel with broken eggshells and a smooth, round pebble with a hole in the top of it.

Nothing to explain the awful smell or the sensations.

What on earth had brought all that on?

Armado was sitting cross-legged and silent in front of her but at a slight distance now. He looked shocked and puzzled. Or was it more like suspicious?

"Lightheaded. Not enough lunch perhaps?" Vanessa offered up weakly.

Armado didn't even bother to reply. She knew he was waiting for a real explanation. Should she make up some story about having epilepsy or something? But if she did that, Frida would be onto her father like a shot, and she would be sent home before she could work out what was going on.

"Sorry. I'm really not sure what happened there." Better to be honest—well, honest-ish—Vanessa decided. "I just felt sort of funny, and then I think I passed out. Probably scary for you, though."

Armado didn't reply to that, but he offered his hand to help her to her feet.

"Do you feel well enough to go?" he asked. "The rain is less now. We must not be late for dinner," he added, almost to himself.

"But we just got here. It can't be anywhere near dinner time yet."

"Vanessa, it's eight o'clock already, and we still have a long ride back."

"How long have we been here?"

"Well, I have been here about forty minutes, Vanessa, but I am not sure about you."

Vanessa opened her mouth to try and protest but suddenly found it difficult to speak. How was she going to manage the ride home?

"I think we should tell Mama about this. You probably should see a doctor."

"No!" Vanessa gasped. "Please, no, Armado. You know they will all worry and fuss, and I may even get sent home if they think I'm sick. Please?" she pleaded.

She smiled the best smile she could as proof of her health and sanity while not at all sure of it herself. She could see the uncertainty in his face.

"Sometimes I just get these visions, it's to do with the place rather than me."

Vanessa was certain she had made it worse, been too honest. They would be calling in a doctor all right—a shrink! But to her surprise it had the opposite effect on Armado, and he nodded his head slowly as if it made everything clearer.

"*Si, alucinación.* I know some people get them,

especially shamans." He stopped and pressed his lips together.

"Shamans?"

"Holy men, like priests," Armado said shortly.

"Oh, yes," said Vanessa. "They do magic, don't they?"

"OK, Vanessa, I will say nothing. Mama and Papa are worried enough at the moment. About the ranch, I mean. This rain is good, but we do not know if it will continue."

Vanessa didn't reply. She was too busy enjoying the remarkable feeling of Armado's hand wrapped firmly around her own as he led her out of the house.

CHAPTER 9

In spite of its fondness for killing goats, the Chupacabra has also been accused of killing birds, chickens, pigs, horses, and cows.

The storm raged all day and all night, bringing down many large trees on the property. However, the great start to the rainy season turned out to be a false one, as the next morning the sun came out in a cloudless sky and not one more drop of rain fell during the girls' stay on the ranch.

There were no more riding lessons that week, and

Vanessa saw very little of Armado or Joseph over the next few days, not even at meal times. She felt that the tension in the house was greater than usual.

"Something's up, don't you think?" Vanessa said to Nikki as they sat on the terrace outside their bedrooms one afternoon. Neither of the girls could get used to the siesta thing. Xolo was sitting at Vanessa's feet.

"How do you mean?" said Nikki.

"Well, can't you feel it? Like everyone is walking around on eggshells," Vanessa said, stroking Xolo's head.

"It's probably because of the cow that died yesterday. One of the ranch hands found it after they went out to check storm damage. Everyone was very upset about it."

"Well, that's not exactly a disaster, is it? I think they have another two thousand four hundred and ninety-nine left. So what's the big deal?"

"I don't know, Vanessa. I suppose it is their livelihood," Nikki said shortly.

"Maybe it has something to do with the curse thing again. You remember Carmen said that the locals call it Devil Ranch? And that the animals die in a strange way?"

"I remember Carmen didn't want to talk about it, all right."

Nikki sounded irritated, and Vanessa felt a sudden pang of jealousy. Vanessa was a good friend, but Carmen was family, after all. The cousins were becoming very close these days.

"I have to go." Nikki stood up. "Embroidery at three o'clock. On the dot." Nikki smiled. "You're much happier in the kitchen with Izel, aren't you?" she added.

"Absolutely. Izel is wonderful. Maybe I'll ask her about the cow and how it died."

"Oh, for God's sake, Vanessa, you are like a dog with a bone," Nikki said.

A bone? Xolo looked up quickly and put his tongue out. The girls laughed together.

"That's one clever dog," Vanessa said, standing up. Xolo stood up to follow her. "No, Xolo. You can't come to the kitchen. Remember last time?"

Xolo sat down again.

"My God, he really does understand you!" Nikki said in amazement. "What happened in the kitchen last time?"

Vanessa hadn't told Nikki about the face at the

window and the fright she got. "I'll tell you later," she promised.

Izel was cracking eggs into a huge bowl when Vanessa arrived in the kitchen.

"What are we making today?" Vanessa asked.

"A cake." Izel pointed to the bowl. "Ten cups of butter, one of goose fat, fifteen of brown sugar, a cup of honey, almonds and cherries soaked for two days in brandy, twenty cups of flour and thirteen eggs."

"Thirteen eggs! Mum used to use three in hers." Izel shrugged her fat shoulders. "You're in Mexico now. We like everything big here."

"My mum died two years ago," Vanessa said quietly. She wanted Izel to know.

"Yes, *chica*, Frida told me. She told me before you arrive."

Frida? Who had told *her*? Not Vanessa's father, surely?

"Was she pretty, like you?" asked Izel.

Vanessa was overwhelmed for a moment by a flood of affection, and she put her arms halfway around the small woman's large waist and hugged her hard.

"I'm not pretty, Izel. But she was. Clever too." Izel started to sieve the flour into the mixture.

"People are always scared to talk to me about my mother. As if they don't want to remind me. But I want to remember now. I think about her every day. At first it was hard, too painful, but Nessie—sorry . . ." She coughed to allow herself some time to think. "But someone helped me through the roughest part. It's easier for me now."

She needn't have worried about Izel peppering her with questions or staring at her the way Frida did.

"She will always be close to you. Especially if you are in difficulty," Izel said, still busy with the cake.

Incredible. Here was a stranger from the other side of the world who understood exactly how she felt.

"You know, my headmistress called me into her office after Mum died and told me that 'time will heal.'"

Izel stopped what she was doing and thought for a moment. "It is true that if your knee is hurt time will heal it, but what has it got to do with your mama dying?"

Vanessa grinned. "Exactly! Time doesn't make those feelings go away; it just changes them a little. The wound is still there."

As she said it, the word "wound" triggered another thought for Vanessa.

"Izel, what happened to the animal that died in the storm yesterday?"

Izel didn't reply immediately. "There was more than one. They were attacked, their lifeblood drained from them. *Es el diablo.*"

The devil again.

"It sounds more like the Chupacabra to me," said Vanessa lightly.

Izel's head shot up. "It is the same thing," she said, her voice lower and harder than usual. She looked frightened to Vanessa. She put her finger to her lips. A silent warning.

Vanessa was rooted to the spot. What was Izel trying to tell her? Did she believe in the Chupacabra? Had she seen it? Before Vanessa could ask her any questions, the kitchen door opened and Armado's face appeared around it.

"Is it safe to come in?" he asked.

Vanessa wondered if he had heard them talking about the Chupacabra or if it was some long-standing joke that he shared with Izel.

Izel wiped her hands on the front of her apron and opened her arms wide for him to hug her. Adoration was the only word for it.

"Mado, Mado, *ven acqui*."

Armado allowed himself to be pressed to her chest, her wrestler's arms enveloping him although he towered over her. He grinned at Vanessa over the top of Izel's head.

"I make your favorite—cherry brandy fool cake," Izel cooed.

"You eat too much cake, you get drunk, and you behave like a fool," Armado explained to Vanessa with a grin. "Well, that is what her husband did when she made it, so that's its name. But you won't find it in any recipe book, I promise you. It's an Izel special."

Vanessa smiled, but the word "fool" had brought back a flood of memories of their ride and her funny turn in the house, and Vanessa felt her tongue tie itself in knots.

Armado dipped his finger in the cake mix and licked it clean, drawing a torrent of Spanish from Izel. Vanessa recognized the words *caballos* and *sucio*: horses and dirty. She smiled. That pretty much summed Armado up; he was always covered in a layer of ranch dust. Vanessa was pleased that she understood Izel. Even after a week her Spanish was definitely improving.

"I just came in to see if you and Nikki wanted to come to Guanajuato tomorrow morning to get some supplies."

Vanessa was relieved. He wouldn't have asked if he really thought that she was a mental case or that she might go all faint on him again, would he?

"That would be fantastic; we'd love to."

"Papa said to tell you to be ready about ten-thirty tomorrow."

Papa. Of course, it was Joseph who was really asking them, not Armado. Vanessa had a fleeting moment of disappointment, but she nodded her agreement to the arrangement and smiled.

"Don't eat too much fool cake before I see you again," Armado said over his shoulder as he walked out of the kitchen.

Vanessa stared after him, her brain a scramble of emotions. What was that supposed to mean? She seemed to waver between liking Armado a lot one minute and wanting to punch him the next.

CHAPTER 10

On Saturday 29 April 2000, Joseph Ismael Pino, a farm worker, saw the Chupacabra. He is reported to have said that "it hardly moved. It just stood there looking at me. It stood upright, five feet tall, with long clawed arms, enormous fangs protruding from its mouth."

"I don't know what's wrong with Xolo," Carmen said. "I've never seen him like this. He's moping around you all the time. What have you done to him, Vanessa?"

The three girls, who were sitting on Carmen's bed, looked down at the dog lying on the floor, his head on his front paws. As if on cue, he raised his head and fixed his eyes directly on Vanessa.

"He's in love!" Nikki threw a pillow at Vanessa. Vanessa threw it back hard, throwing herself after it so that they fell off the bed and almost flattened the dog. There was a knock on the door.

"Carmen, *que es*? What is all that noise?" Frida's sharp voice made them all jump.

"*Lo siento*, Mama, sorry. My book fell off the bed onto the floor."

Vanessa and Nikki shoved their faces into their pillows to mute their giggles, amazed by Carmen's quick lie.

"It is already ten o'clock, Carmen; it is time you slept."

Vanessa prayed that Frida would not open the door and see them on the floor in such a state. It would be just too embarrassing.

"Good night, Mama," Carmen called.

"*Buenos noches, Carmencita, te quiero*. Love you . . ." Vanessa was surprised at the loving way Frida had spoken. It was enough to make her stop giggling.

They waited until Frida's footsteps died away and then got back up on the bed. They had calmed down now and neither Nikki nor Vanessa knew what to say.

Carmen did not notice that they were feeling uncomfortable. "You're lucky to be such close friends," she said. She brushed the hair off her forehead and looked wistful.

Vanessa felt sorry for her. How lonely it must be for Carmen on the ranch. Frida was not exactly fun, and Armado and Joseph were not around much. It struck her that Carmen never talked about school or visiting friends.

Vanessa yawned. It was getting late and they had an early start in the morning.

"How far away is Guanajuato, Carmen?" Vanessa asked.

"About twelve miles, but the roads are small and twisty so it takes time. Mado and Papa usually ride, but I suppose he wants to show off the town to you two, so we will go by car."

"Good. I don't think my riding skills would be up to that yet," said Vanessa.

"Mado says you are a wonderful rider," Carmen replied.

Nikki arched her eyebrows quizzically. As a distraction, Vanessa quickly launched into the story about the storm and how they had had to take shelter in the derelict house.

"You didn't go inside, did you?" Carmen sounded alarmed.

"Yes. Into the room that's always dry."

Vanessa was beginning to wish she hadn't started. Clearly Armado hadn't mentioned going there or told Carmen about her funny turn.

Nikki looked puzzled. "A room that is always dry. Well, why wouldn't it be if it's in a house?"

"Yes, but it's a wet house." Vanessa was using a silly sort of voice to make fun of it. "This one room is always dry, although there is almost no roof and the rest of the house leaks like a sieve."

Carmen's face remained serious.

"Mado should not have taken you there. He knows we are forbidden to go there." She spoke vehemently, and Vanessa could see how upset she was. What was it with that house? Vanessa tried to keep her breathing even, reluctant to remember the sensations that had overwhelmed her that day.

"Why?" said Vanessa. "Tell me why, Carmen."

"Could someone please fill me in?" Nikki bleated. "Please?"

"*Malvado* lives there now," said Carmen quietly.

"Malvado?" Vanessa asked. "Is that one of the locals?"

"No, *malvado* means evil in Spanish," Nikki said. "Now will you stop talking and tell me what happened?"

At that moment, Vanessa could not speak even if she had known what exactly had happened. Her throat and chest were constricted so tight that they pained her.

"A local, one of the Nahua, used to live in that house," said Carmen. "I think he was the shaman—a good man. But he disappeared and then evil moved in."

"Disappeared?" said Nikki, her eyes wide.

"When did that happen?" asked Vanessa. "When did he disappear?"

"About four years ago," Carmen replied. "Just before we came to the ranch."

Before they came to the ranch? Vanessa's mind was racing. Joseph had told her that the ranch had been in the family for generations. It wasn't adding up.

"And has anything else strange happened since then?" asked Nikki.

Carmen shook her head slowly.

"Well, that doesn't sound too bad. Maybe the shaman just moved somewhere else, maybe to a better house." Nikki would always look for the sensible solution.

"That is what Mado says." But Carmen was clearly not reassured. "Don't ever say to Mama that he took you there. Anyway, it's late. I think we need to get some sleep now." Carmen was determined to bring the conversation to an end.

CHAPTER 11

While lots of tribes used to be head hunters, the Amazonian tribe called the Jivaro are the only people in the world to have shrunk human heads. In their culture a shrunken head is called a *tsantsa* and has significant powers.

Back in her own room, Vanessa dug deep in her rucksack and pulled out her shrunken head. It was a strange thing to have, but it was one of her most treasured possessions. Its tiny face was wizened but in perfect proportion, and it was small enough to fit into the palm of her hand.

Vanessa stared at the head, willing it to open its eyes and speak to her. The twine stitches across the eyelids and lips were a little grotesque, maybe, but the shrunken head fascinated her. It had originally belonged to her grandfather Todd—she called it Toddy, after him—and then to her mother. Vanessa had found it in the attic with her mother's Cryptid Files. It was like a good-luck charm for her, and she brought it everywhere, even to school in her bag, although she never showed it to anybody, not even to Nikki.

Usually holding it had the effect of calming her, of allowing her to think and sometimes even to find answers to impossible questions. She held it now, hoping it would inspire her to understand what was going on, but her mind was a frustrating blank.

"What's going on here?" she whispered to Toddy. Something was wrong. Was she the only one who felt it, or did others notice it? Izel certainly knew something. Frida, too?

Sometimes Vanessa tried to imagine the person whose head this had been. She wondered about his age, his tribe. Head-shrinking was done to paralyze the spirit of the dead, she knew, so that they could not seek revenge on their killer. The Jivaro tribe, the people who made shrunken heads like this, had absolute belief in the power of the dead over the living, the power of the spiritual world over the physical one. Sometimes Vanessa felt as if she was caught somewhere between the two worlds herself.

A scratching noise startled her, and she sat up in bed, her heart fluttering in her chest. The whine that followed made her laugh, and she flopped back onto the bed again. She imagined Xolo lying outside her bedroom door. Guarding her. She felt safer with him there. *But safe from what?* she asked the head. No answer.

Then it struck her that there was someone else who knew what was going on in this place. Well, not exactly "someone" —Xolo. That dog had behaved strangely since she'd arrived. If only she could really talk to animals in the way that Armado teased her about.

Vanessa tucked the shrunken head under her pillow. She looked at her watch. It was two in the morning and she wanted to sleep, but her thoughts kept running in circles.

She imagined what her brothers Luke and Ronan were doing at home at that moment; where her dad and his girlfriend, Lee, were. Lee had been a good friend to Vanessa since their visit to Loch Ness, and as a zoologist she knew a lot about animals. Maybe Vanessa should call Lee and ask her about the Chupacabra.

Her thoughts moved on to the shaman's house. Had Armado deliberately brought her there? Who was the shaman and where had he gone?

Sleep. She would have to get some sleep. She put her hand beneath the pillow and held the head again. Could it really be hotter? It certainly seemed to be. Were her own feverish imaginings infecting it? She threw back the sheet to cool herself down.

She didn't understand it! Why was the shrunken head not having its usual calming effect? If she didn't slow her mind down it just might burst into flames.

She could just imagine the headlines: "Irish schoolgirl sets bed on fire; ranch burns to the ground." Or "Brain fever sweeps through central Mexico—locals suspect that *el diablo* is at the center of it all."

Stop it!

She got up and washed her face with cold water and brushed her hair until the roots hurt. Then she lay down again and watched the ceiling fan above her bed rotating slowly. She forced herself to think of embroidery, the needle making stitches—that would send her to sleep. It took a while, but finally her eyes grew heavy.

"I'm just imagining things again, Toddy," she whispered sleepily.

Maybe not, the head replied under the pillow, but Vanessa had already fallen into a deep, untroubled sleep.

CHAPTER 12

On Wednesday 12 May 1996, in Mexico's southern state of Chiapas, 28 dead rams were found with puncture wounds in their bodies.

"Here they come," Carmen announced as an army-style jeep scuttled and bumped down the track toward the girls. It was surrounded by a halo of red dust.

"Hop in the back there, girls," Joseph shouted through the open window. Despite all his years living in Mexico, his Irish accent still came through quite strongly sometimes.

Once they were in, the jeep shot off at speed. Sitting in the middle, Vanessa felt a knobbly elbow dig painfully into her ribs from Nikki's side. She turned to her, about to protest, but her friend was surreptitiously pointing to Armado. He was sitting in the front seat beside Joseph. Nikki made a discreet driving motion with an imaginary steering wheel, and it took Vanessa a couple of seconds to realize what she was getting at. Of course, the wheel was on the opposite side of the car—and Armado was driving. Wasn't fifteen young to have a license, even in Mexico?

When Vanessa looked up again, she caught a pair of dark eyes in the front mirror watching her. She knew at once that Armado must have seen her making faces at Nikki, but she couldn't read his expression. Being caught like that made her temper flare, and she was tempted to tell him to keep his eyes on the road in the future. But a shout from outside broke their gaze, and the truck skidded to a halt.

Vanessa was horrified. It was the same mean face that had scared her at the kitchen window. Now that face was coming through the open car window, right at her. Vanessa reacted instantly, clutching Nikki's hand and shrinking back into her seat.

She prayed feverishly that he wouldn't get into the car. If he did, she would have to get out, and that would be very difficult to explain.

His long hair was tied back this time, but his dead eyes, oversized mouth, and disgusting teeth were the same. He smiled a cruel smile. He rested his long, skinny arms along the open window and leaned in. Vanessa looked away.

"Hey, Pablo. *¿Necesita usted un aventón?* Need a lift?" Armado asked.

They spoke for no more than twenty seconds, but to Vanessa it was agony. She held her breath, and the skin on her arms and neck prickled.

Pull yourself together, she told herself sternly. The man was ugly and looked threatening, but he had done nothing except stare through a couple of windows. He was definitely creepy, but that wasn't exactly a crime. Vanessa looked around at everybody else. They didn't seem bothered.

Armado finally put his foot on the accelerator and sped off without Pablo. Vanessa's relief was so strong that she slumped back in her seat and closed her eyes.

"What's wrong, Vanessa?" Nikki asked.

Joseph turned in his seat, his large, ruddy face full

of concern.

"OK, Vanessa?"

Vanessa smiled at him, annoyed with herself at her overreaction. What on earth was the matter with her?

"Yes, I'm fine, honestly. I just got dust in my eye, that's all," she said, rubbing her face to make sure that any suspicion of tears was removed.

Armado's eyes were trained on her once more in the mirror. How many pairs of eyes did he have, and did they always have to be watching her? She swallowed. The dryness of her throat made it difficult, but she had to ask.

"Who was that, Joseph?"

"Oh, that's Pablo, one of the oldest ranch hands. He's lived here for over thirty years."

"Is he the one you said was good with horses, Armado?" Vanessa lifted her eyes to look in the mirror and was unreasonably disappointed that Armado was watching the road now.

"No, that is Cesar. Pablo is much better with machinery than animals," Armado replied with a strange laugh.

"How do—" Vanessa started but then stopped as the car lurched violently, catapulting the girls along the back seat to one side and summoning a chorus of screeches. The lurch out of the large pothole was equally violent, the wheels spinning furiously as the car found its way back onto the track.

"*Muy bien*. Well done, me boyo." Joseph tapped his son proudly on the shoulder as Armado drove on calmly.

Vanessa and Nikki could not explain to Carmen quite why they found Joseph's remarks so funny. But the odd mix of Mexican and Irish struck them as hilarious, and they dissolved into a heap of giggles in the back seat.

For the moment, Pablo was entirely forgotten.

CHAPTER 13

Jaime Cruz, a 21-year-old shepherd from Irapuato, Guanajuato, saw the strange beast several times between Ejido Curva de Juan Sánchez and the Colinas de Santiago district. It was no ordinary animal, he said, and was capable of extremely high leaps.

Once they reached the main road and were off the Martinez property, Joseph took over the driving. He drove much more slowly than Armado and didn't look in the rearview mirror at all.

The town of Guanajuato was wedged in the very

bottom of a deep ravine, like a small cherry stuck at the bottom of an ice-cream sundae glass. It was backed by huge, barren mountains and smooth, high cliffs which entirely dwarfed the town. The road wiggled its way down into the center, going underground for many miles.

The roads were narrow and busy, and their progress slow. It was hot in the car. The open windows were the only air-conditioning, and Vanessa found that her legs had stuck to the plastic seats. Why hadn't she worn longer shorts like Carmen or a dress like Nikki? She tried to shift in her seat but found she was stuck fast. It was going to hurt when she tried to separate her skin from it. She hoped it wouldn't make an embarrassing sound too.

Finally they reached the town center, and Joseph pulled up in the middle of the road. He turned in his seat, totally unfazed by the chorus of loud horns and beeps that started up from behind and provided the perfect cover for the unsticking of Vanessa's legs.

"Mado and I have to go to Don Arias for an hour, so we'll drop you guys off here and meet you in the Jardín de la Unión. You know where that is, Carmen." At eleven o'clock in the morning the town was already busy. Groups of very old women sat around on wooden benches. They had string shopping bags and were huddled in groups, talking, heads bent close. Vanessa could almost imagine the cauldron bubbling between them.

Vanessa spotted the sign first: "*Se vende helado.*" Ice cream for sale. Already too hot, they stopped in front of the extraordinary display of ice cream flavors that stretched the width of the glass-fronted shop. In Dublin, ice cream either meant a soft-serve cone from Teddy's on the seafront in Sandycove or a bar from the bottom of a freezer in the local shop. Here vats of different flavors were lined up side by side in endless rows. Carmen translated the flavors—squashed raspberry, vanilla with chips of Brazil nut, guava and sour cream, crushed mango with spicy ginger.

The girls chose their ice creams and sat down under an umbrella at the wooden table and chairs in front of the shop. Vanessa leaned back, nibbling at her orange and dark chocolate cone while Carmen and Nikki chatted away, their words drifting by her on the warm air.

Coming up a side alley onto the plaza, a group of guitar players dressed in velvet breeches were trailed by spectators. They were all singing.

More fancy dress, thought Vanessa, remembering the bird woman at the airport. She had a beak. But of course it was a mask. It must have been.

"*Callejoneadas.*" Carmen laughed.

"What's that?" asked Vanessa. "The funny clothes they are wearing?"

"No," said Carmen. "It is having a street party. *Calle* means alleyway, see?"

Nikki giggled. "It's a bit different from Dun Laoghaire or Dundrum, isn't it, Vanessa?"

It was Carmen who answered. "Is it? I'd love to visit Ireland. I'd love to see Europe: Paris, Rome, Barcelona," she said with longing. "I'm going to go to university in Spain, if Mama will let me."

"What will you study?" Vanessa looked at Carmen's slim hands and perfectly groomed nails and compared them to her own short, bitten ones.

"I have no idea. I just want to live in Europe," Carmen answered honestly. "Mama will probably not let me go, though."

"Oh, difficult parents can be won over if you want something enough," Vanessa tried to reassure her. Her dad was not a pushover, but Frida was much tougher. Vanessa secretly wondered about the possibility of changing Frida's mind about anything at all.

At noon, as arranged, they met Armado at the corner of the square.

"Why don't we show them *Callejon del Beso*, Armado?" Carmen suggested.

"*Calle* what?" said Vanessa. "An alleyway?"

"Alley of the kiss," said Carmen, kissing the air. "It brings good luck to kiss your beloved there. Maybe you could try it out, Vanessa—you and Armado."

"Shut up, Carmen," muttered Armado. Vanessa's face was on fire.

"But we always bring guests there, Armado," Carmen blundered on. "It's very famous."

Nikki giggled at the idea of a street for kissing in, but Vanessa just wished they would all shut up about it.

"I think Vanessa and Nikki might prefer to go to the museum, Carmen."

A museum? The girls had quite fancied finding a market and doing a bit of shopping.

"No, Mado, *por favor, no me gusta*," Carmen pleaded. "I hate that place."

Vanessa looked at her in surprise. What kind of a museum would be that bad?

CHAPTER 14

The Mummy Museum is a famous attraction in Guanajuato. Fifty-nine mummies that were dug up in the late 1800s are on display there. There are men, women and children, some of them still in original dress with their hair and teeth intact. It is the largest collection of mummies anywhere in the Western Hemisphere.

"*Museo de las Momias* is so interesting," Armado argued. "They are real mummies, Vanessa. I think you would love it."

"I thought you only got mummies in Egypt,"

Vanessa said.

"Well, they are a different kind of mummy, perhaps; not man-made. They are natural, so to speak. Two hundred years ago there was not enough room for all the dead bodies, you see, so they dug up the old ones to make space. But the bodies had not become skeletons. They still have their hair, teeth, clothes . . ."

"How come?" asked Vanessa.

"Some people think it is witchcraft." Armado shrugged.

"And others?" Vanessa prompted him.

"Others think it is maybe strange soil conditions here. Maybe the arsenic that is naturally in the ground of the silver mines preserves the bodies."

"A lot more likely," Vanessa said. "It sounds like fun to me." And it was certainly better than standing, mortified, in the kissing alley!

• •

Carmen grabbed hold of Nikki's hand as they joined the queue outside the museum. There were street sellers everywhere. Women and children crouching on the ground held up boxes of chewing gum, trays with carved wooden turtles, fake Ralph

Lauren sunglasses and Rolex watches.

A young girl about her own age approached Vanessa and smiled eagerly at her.

"*Ochenta pesos*," she said brightly, showing a small turtle sitting in the center of her small palm. She had brilliant white teeth and a mischievous face, and Vanessa liked her instantly.

Eighty pesos was roughly five euro, she calculated. The turtle was perfect for Ronan. But before she could hand the money over, Carmen began a heated discussion with the young girl. Try as she might, Vanessa could not understand a word being said. They argued for what seemed like an age before Carmen stepped back again.

"Thirty pesos."

Vanessa, slightly stunned, handed over a hundred peso note. "Maybe I'll take two, then. *Dos?*" she said meekly to the girl, who rewarded her with a huge smile.

"You are expected to bargain here, Vanessa. You must never accept the first price." Carmen explained as they walked away.

"What language did you speak to her, Carmen? It wasn't Spanish, was it?"

"An old language, Nahuatl. It was what they spoke before the Spanish came. Some people still speak it. Like Izel and Mama. Armado and I learned a little when we were growing up."

"Wow. Impressive!"

"Not really. Most of our Nahua words are related to cooking. Luckily turtle soup is one of Izel's favorite recipes," Carmen said with a smile.

• •

At first Vanessa was delighted with the displays of mummified bodies. She smiled to herself, thinking of the small shrunken head that she carried in her backpack.

Armado translated a plaque: "The first mummy was found in 1865; his name was Dr. Remigio Leroy, a French doctor."

Vanessa looked at the dead man, still in his overcoat, his mouth stretched in a gargoyle-style grin.

"There was also a woman buried alive," Armado said, and they moved to the next display. She was lying down with her hands clutched in front of her, horror etched in the sinewy remains. Vanessa swallowed hard. The backlighting made the bodies look really eerie. She heard Nikki's sharp intake of breath.

"Oh, the poor thing," Nikki murmured. "What a way to die."

Vanessa noticed that Carmen stared off into the distance to avoid looking directly at any of the mummies.

As the others moved ahead through the crowded museum, Vanessa began to feel a growing sense of unease. Somewhere in the middle of the second room, her heart took off and she found it harder and harder to look at the mummies' faces. The empty eye sockets were really freaky. In front of her she saw Nikki's blonde head and Carmen's dark one bobbing in and out of the crowd. She should catch up to them.

She looked around for Armado. He was standing in front of a mummy of a young child. As Vanessa approached it, avoiding its eyes, she saw, to her horror, the child's bony foot slowly turning into an animal's paw. It was as if a two-ton weight had landed on her chest. The air that was expelled from her came out as a loud groan.

Vanessa moved away quickly, but she came face to face with another mummy. This time the wizened, gaping mouth became the mouth of a snake, and she saw a black tongue that whipped from side to side.

Vanessa's scream was small and choked, and she clamped her hands to her mouth. Trembling, she felt tears gathering in the corners of her eyes. She had to get out of here. Where was the exit? She pushed her way toward Nikki and Carmen.

"Look at this one, Vanessa," Nikki said as she came up to her. "It's so sad. A tiny baby who was buried with her mother."

Vanessa couldn't bear to look. She just didn't know what she might see.

"Vanessa, you're not looking," Nikki persisted.

If no one else was seeing these things, it must be all in her imagination—and then she could control it, couldn't she? She forced herself to look.

Before her eyes, the baby mummy became a tiny monkey clinging to its mother's arm.

Vanessa backed away hurriedly. Her legs felt weak, and she dropped down onto one knee. She could hear people talking but not the words. Were they talking about her? She tried to calm herself as she retied her shoelace.

Somebody touched her shoulder.

"Are you coming, Vanessa?" Armado had joined them and wanted to move on.

"Yeah, with you in a minute. You go on."

Vanessa's voice sounded wobbly, and she prayed that he wouldn't notice. She knelt on her other knee and retied that lace slowly. The shaman's house had been bad enough; what would he think if she freaked out again?

Vanessa waited till they had gone ahead and then stood up carefully. Her jelly legs appeared to be holding her weight, although she couldn't imagine how. Looking neither right nor left, she made her way outside somehow. It was all she could do to lower herself without collapsing on the side of the pavement. She covered her eyes with her hands, but the tears kept coming. After a bit she felt her panic begin to subside. She would have to get her act together before the others came out.

A slight pressure on one of her hands made her jump, and she jerked upright. Vanessa found herself staring into the face of the young girl who had sold her the turtles not half an hour earlier.

"Naguaaaaal," she hissed, pushing something into Vanessa's hand.

The girl ran off quickly.

Vanessa stared at the long, gray . . . tooth that had been pressed into the palm of her hand. What was that word? *Nagwaal*? Was it the word for tooth in the girl's language or something? And what on earth was she supposed to do with it?

Vanessa wiped her tears with the back of her other hand to get a better look at the tooth. It looked like an animal's canine, certainly way too big to be a human tooth. Maybe she should ask the girl. Vanessa hopped to her feet and looked around for her, but she had long since disappeared into the crowd.

CHAPTER 15

Nagual comes from the Nahuatl word for "disguise." Naguals are people who can shapeshift at night into small animals—typically a dog, coyote, bat or turkey—and suck the blood of their victims.

Vanessa sat in the back of the jeep fidgeting, her palms and the back of her neck damp with sweat. She hoped that the others would appear soon. She had told Joseph that, like Carmen, she had found the mummies a bit freaky and that was why she had left the museum before the others. Luckily he hadn't seen her bawling her eyes out on the pavement.

"Is there an Internet café in Guanajuato?" Vanessa asked now.

Joseph was in the process of downing a can of Coke in one swallow. He finished it before answering.

"Yup. Do you need to use it?"

"That would be great. I promised to send an email to Dad and the boys when I spoke to them the other evening. You don't have Internet at the ranch?" Vanessa knew the answer already.

"Not Frida's thing, really," Joseph replied breezily. "Oh, look, here come the others now."

The Internet café was absolutely tiny with no windows. Instead of a door there was just a curtain of beaded strings. How did they lock the shop up at night? Vanessa wondered.

Luckily there were plenty of terminals available, and the three girls took their seats. Armado had decided to go to the bar with Joseph and meet them back at the truck later.

The first word she typed into the search engine was *nagwaal*.

Above the results list, the question "Do you mean

nagual?" prompted her. So that was how you spelled it. She opened up the first item.

A nagual is a type of brujo, or witch. It is a shape-shifter who can take on the body of an animal. They are the powerful ones in a community, usually evil and greatly feared. Ordinary people can't necessarily identify naguals in their community, but naguals can recognize each other.

Vanessa froze. Shapeshifters? Someone turning into something else? Hadn't she just seen dead bodies turn into animals at the museum? And what about the woman who turned into a bird at the airport?

And what about naguals being able to recognize each other? Did that mean the young girl was one and thought Vanessa was one too? Could she be one without knowing it? Maybe that was why she was having all these strange visions. Except she wasn't the one turning into an animal—she was seeing others shapeshifting. That was different. Wasn't it?

Carmen had said that the turtle girl spoke the local language. Maybe it had something to do with that Mexican tribe, the one that Izel belonged to.

Nahwha, wasn't it?

Once again the computer corrected her. Nahua.

The Nahua people in Mexico date back to pre-Columbian times and are considered the direct descendants of the Aztecs. They mostly live in central Mexico, and it is estimated that 1.4 million people speak the language Nahuatl. They are amongst the many tribes in Mexico that practice shamanism. The traditional Mexican shaman is a powerful individual within the community who has magical and spiritual powers that come directly from supernatural beings through spirit possession, visions, and dreams.

The shaman. The shaman just kept on coming up somehow. Was there a connection?

"We have about ten minutes before we meet Mado and Papa."

Vanessa was concentrating so hard on the screen that Carmen's words barely registered. She had one last word to look up. Izel had given her the correct spelling.

The xolo (pronounced sholo) is a rare hairless dog native to Mexico. As a breed these dogs have been around for three

thousand years and were considered sacred by the Aztecs,
who used to eat their meat. In some parts of rural Mexico
the meat is still sold, although it is against the law.

Vanessa stared at the screen, her heart quickening
beneath her breastbone. Yuck! How could people eat
a dog? No wonder Xolo was wary of people.

The xolo is known to be an excellent watchdog, but it is also
thought to have curative powers, curing rheumatism and
fevers as well as protecting against evil spirits . . .

Vanessa stopped reading. She saw from the corner
of her eye that Carmen had stood up and gone over to
Nikki's computer.

If Vanessa was going to email Lee, she would have
to do it quickly. Her father's girlfriend was the only
person in the world whom Vanessa could tell about
her visions. Maybe Lee might be able to help her
understand what was going on at the ranch.

Vanessa's fingers hovered above the keys. How
would she start? Best just to ask it straight out. She
glanced at Carmen who was leaning over Nikki's
shoulder, laughing at some pictures on Facebook.

Hi Lee. Hope Finland is cool. Having a great time and will tell you all soon but first I have a question for you. A strange one. Since Loch Ness, have you ever had hallucinations? Well, I have. Three times in Mexico—first at the airport a woman changed into a bird. The second time it happened in an old house that belonged to a local shaman who has disappeared. Too weird to explain. But the third time and THE WORST happened just now at the mummy museum. These really dead people changed before my eyes into animals—well, bits of them. There is no one else I can tell. Am I going mad? Is it—

"Are you finished, Vanessa? We will need to pay now if we want to meet up with Mado."

Vanessa was aware of Carmen standing behind her and panicked. She pressed the send button quickly without signing off, praying that Carmen hadn't read it. Oh God. What would Lee think of her email ending in the middle like that?

CHAPTER 16

Naguals look like ordinary people but have supernatural powers. These abilities can be learned from another nagual and are often passed down through families.

The girls' Spanish lessons began the next morning. Lambs to the slaughter, they were led into Frida's study. It was a beautiful room with full-length windows and large oil paintings on the walls. Vanessa knew better than to comment on them.

Frida pointed to a couple of chairs that were on

the opposite side of her desk, which was huge and covered with small towers of books. She handed two books to the girls. They were children's picture books in Spanish—much more interesting than the textbooks they had expected. Things were looking up just a fraction.

"You will first read these simple books in Spanish and then translate them for me," Frida said shortly.

"*Lea*, Nikki, *por favor*. Read, Nikki, please.'

The girls were getting used to Frida's curt ways. Vanessa had never met anyone so tense and closed-up, and yet her clothes were so wild. Today her hair was tied back loosely with a red scarf, and she wore several silver bangles which jangled on her wrists. Her plain black dress had a multicolored silk shawl with a long fringe tied around her waist. It was ten o'clock in the morning and she looked as if she was going flamenco dancing rather than teaching.

Vanessa leafed through the book she had been given. It was beautifully illustrated but seemed to be a really sad story. A child's face was reflected in a window as she looked through it. A fire in the hearth on one side contrasted with a gloomy scene outside.

Nikki read her book out loud as Frida had asked

and then translated it. It seemed to come easily to her. There was no way Vanessa was going to do as well as that.

Frida folded her hands in her lap, and when she had finished correcting Nikki's pronunciation she turned to Vanessa.

"*Dibujas*, Vanessa?" When Vanessa shrugged her shoulders noncommittally Frida repeated the question, in English this time. "Do you draw?"

"Yes. But not like this," Vanessa answered, pointing to the illustration. "This is amazing, so atmospheric. But I do sketches sometimes."

"Vanessa's really good," Nikki cut in. "She's the best artist in the class. No, the best in our whole year, actually."

"*Muy bien*," said Frida, smiling warmly.

Vanessa was taken aback. Frida did not often smile. The last time was when she had been talking to Izel. Maybe she was interested in art? Vanessa's eyes flicked to the paintings on the walls. Could Frida have painted them? Vanessa still didn't dare ask.

"Maybe you could draw a picture for our next class and we could make up a story about it in Spanish," Frida suggested.

"OK," Vanessa agreed reluctantly. There was no polite way out of this, really. "I'll give it a try, but it might take me a couple of days."

"*Hablamos solo español, por favor,*" Frida said. She wanted them to speak in Spanish only. An hour of this every day and her Spanish would certainly improve. Vanessa was trying her best to think positive.

Later that day Vanessa drew a load of different pictures but was happy with none of them. Now she sat in front of a pencil sketch of "her" horse, Amigo, and stared at it critically.

"How can you say that's a bad drawing, Vanessa?" Nikki said impatiently.

Vanessa had spent ages on it after her riding lesson with Armado that afternoon. Things were going OK on that front at least. She had had no more weird visions, thankfully, and Armado was teaching her how to jump.

"I suppose it's not bad, but it's not very good either." Vanessa frowned at the drawing.

Nikki pinched her lightly on the hand. "I'd give anything to be able to do that. Just show Frida that one tomorrow and stop agonizing over it. It's only so we can make up a story and practice our Spanish, silly."

The next afternoon, Vanessa brought her sketch-pad to the kitchen when she went to help Izel prepare dinner. It was her favorite part of the day. She loved Izel's stories and the rambling way she told them. Sometimes Izel's accent got so thick that Vanessa had to guess the details; other times she threw in Spanish and Nahuatl words. Vanessa never asked her to explain or translate them because Izel did not like to be interrupted. If she was stopped mid-flow she would often lose the thread of the conversation.

While Izel talked Vanessa tried to sketch her face. She was curious to see if she could catch Izel's good humor and kind heart with her pencil.

Izel sliced and chopped pounds of fresh avocados and onions while Vanessa sat on a stool at the table and sketched.

"Frida drew my face many times," Izel said out of the blue. "She was so clever. At twelve years old she could draw my face and it look like a mirror for me." Her voice lifted and a smile broke her heavy features.

"I was young and beautiful then, like you, Vanessa. In love, too."

Vanessa was shocked. Beautiful and in love? Izel couldn't be talking about her, surely?

"Do you still have the drawings, Izel?" Vanessa changed the subject quickly. "Could I see them?"

Vanessa really wanted to see them. For some strange reason she was pleased to think that Frida was an artist and that they might have something in common. Frida had smiled at her when Nikki mentioned that Vanessa was good at drawing.

"No, Vanessa. They are gone. All gone," Izel said sadly. "She left her pictures in the house when she ran away. When she came back years later they had disappeared. He burned everything, her clothes too."

Vanessa realized that she was holding her breath. Who burned Frida's clothes and pictures? She needed to ask the right question. Otherwise Izel could just as easily start talking about the pork *tabales* she was making for dinner.

"But . . . why, Izel?" Vanessa stuttered slightly.

Then she buttoned her lip firmly and continued to sketch, waiting for Izel to reply.

The silence stretched.

"She was only sixteen and so beautiful," Izel said at last. "She was happy, full of laughing, and foolish but not wicked, as Don Miguel said."

"Don Miguel?" Vanessa prompted Izel.

"That was her father. He said Joseph was a bad man, but Don Miguel was wrong about that too. There was someone else who wanted Frida, you see, and he poisoned Don Miguel's mind. Told him lies about Joseph."

So Frida and Joseph ran away together when they were young! It was hard to imagine Frida doing anything so impulsive.

"That's so romantic!" Vanessa said.

"No, *chica*, so sad. Frida's mother died of her broken heart, and when Frida found out and tried to return to the ranch, her father would not let her. He would not even allow Frida to her own mother's funeral. Imagine such cruelty!"

Izel wiped her eyes with the back of her hand. It was a long time ago, but it was clearly still painful for her.

"Frida, on her knees, begged his forgiveness. But he looked at her, his beautiful daughter that he had loved with passion all of her childhood, and told her that she was dead to him."

It was as if a heavy curtain had been drawn back for just a moment—sunlight streamed in, and Vanessa thought she understood. That was why Frida was so cold and silent now. She had been badly hurt and she probably felt guilty too. What a story! Did Nikki know all this? Vanessa wondered.

She was about to ask if Frida and her father were ever reconciled when Izel slammed down the knife and spoke severely.

"And now we must make the table for seven people tonight."

That meant one extra person. Vanessa was puzzled. "Is somebody coming to dinner?" she asked.

"Yes. But he has not been invited. No one but Don Miguel wanted him in the house back then, and nobody wants him here now."

The curtain closed again.

CHAPTER 17

In May 2007, more than 300 sheep were mysteriously killed in Boyacá, Colombia.

The next afternoon the girls rode the old bikes to the river. They were hoping that the recent storm might have filled the river enough for at least a shallow swim.

They set out lurching and swaying along the dirt track that led to the western part of the ranch. They laughed at each other as they struggled to ride side by side and in a straight line.

Vanessa's bike had a crossbar and was so large that she couldn't put her feet on the ground. Nikki's was more of a giant tricycle and looked as if it had been rescued from a previous century. Carmen's was too small for her, and the handlebars were rusted straight, so she had to keep stopping and repositioning the bike. It was fun.

Izel had prepared a picnic for them, all wrapped up beautifully and packed in a wicker basket. It was strapped to the carrier of Carmen's bike.

"Can I ask you something, Carmen?" Vanessa said as she wobbled from side to side along the track. "Why did Pablo eat dinner with us last night?" Vanessa knew it sounded like a strange question, however she put it. She saw Nikki glancing at her quickly. It probably sounded as if she was being snobbish.

Carmen didn't look at all surprised. She shook her head slowly. "He's horrible, isn't he? Such mean eyes."

"So suspicious of everybody," Vanessa agreed.

"And his teeth! Every time he opens his mouth to eat I have to look away." Carmen's lip curled in distaste.

"Why did Armado say he wasn't very good with animals?" Vanessa asked suddenly. "Remember, in the car to Guanajuato he said that Pablo was much better with machinery than animals?"

"Maybe he is too much of an animal himself and that frightens them," Carmen said, a touch nastily.

Vanessa and Nikki looked at each other in surprise.

"How do you mean, he's an animal, Carmen?" Nikki asked.

"Oh, he's just . . . you know . . . creepy, is how you would say. I don't mean that he's done anything bad. At least not that I've heard anyway. But he's really rude to Mama, and I don't understand why she allows it. She doesn't let anyone else speak to her like that. Armado thinks it has to do with something that happened in the past, but Mama will not speak of it." She paused, looking thoughtful. "And he stares at you, Vanessa, all the time. Have you noticed it?"

Vanessa had been all too aware of Pablo's eyes boring into her at dinner. Even when she refused to meet his gaze, she could still feel his stare.

"But why does Frida invite him to dinner? I know Izel hates him," said Vanessa.

"He doesn't come very often. I don't know why he came yesterday. He knows we don't like him." She paused. "Maybe he wanted to get a good look at you, Vanessa." Carmen was only half-joking.

"Oh, Carmen, don't tease Vanessa like that," said Nikki when she saw the look on Vanessa's face. "He really is horrible."

"Yes, but why is he allowed to come?" Vanessa insisted.

Carmen pulled her sun hat farther down over her eyes and struggled to answer.

"I . . . I think it has something to do with my grandfather's will. I never met Don Miguel, but I know he left Pablo a small house on the ranch. He was only a ranch hand, really, but Don Miguel relied on him, and Pablo used to eat with the family. In his will, my grandfather said Pablo should be welcome at our table always."

"What a strange thing to put in a will!" Vanessa said. "It's the living who have to honor it. That's not really fair."

"Yes, poor Mama. Poor us."

"I wonder why she does honor it, though. Your mother, I mean."

Vanessa stopped and bit her lip. She was probably stepping on very delicate ground here. But Carmen just shrugged. She didn't know.

"I think I'll die if I don't get a swim soon," Nikki grumbled. "It's so hot. Can't we ride on to the river and talk there? And can we talk about something other than Pablo?"

The girls rode on. Vanessa was silent, her mind totally taken over by the mystery of Pablo and why he came to dinner.

They soon arrived at the river. It wasn't deep enough to swim in but the girls lay on the cool stones of the riverbed and let the water run over them. It was crystal clear and felt like heaven after the hot bike ride.

It wasn't until they were sitting on the bank on a rug in the shade that Vanessa was able to bring the conversation back around to Pablo.

"So where does he live on the ranch?" Vanessa said, looking at Carmen. "Pablo, I mean. Where is this house your grandfather left him?"

Nikki rolled her eyes. "So we're back to Pablo, are we? You can be relentless, Vanessa, when you get a bee in your bonnet."

Nikki began to unpack the picnic. Carmen sat up and looked around.

"I think it is near here. It is a small house, somewhere over there," she added, pointing to some trees on the right. "I know it is along this river."

Vanessa's eyes widened. "Let's go and have a look."

"Honestly, Vanessa, you are just downright nosy sometimes," Nikki said. "Well, I'm staying here in the shade and eating this lovely food."

Nikki had set out a bowl of sliced fruit—pineapple and guava. There were also nachos with guacamole and homemade salsa, a bottle of slightly warm hibiscus water, and some giant walnut cookies.

"Maybe we'll go looking after lunch," Vanessa said and reached for a cookie.

After they had eaten, the girls packed up and set off. They followed the riverbank for about ten minutes before they found the place. It was more of a wooden shack than a house, with a corrugated iron roof.

"See, I knew it was on the river. I remember that he always dries his laundry that way." Carmen laughed.

Vanessa stared at the trees surrounding the house. Sheets were drying on one tree, pants on another, and a third was spread with T-shirts. "How strange!" she murmured.

"Actually, lots of people here dry their clothes on trees—though maybe not different trees for different types of clothes. But this is the strange thing: Pablo will only use the river to wash his dishes and his clothes, not the well water."

"Maybe the well water is too low, with the drought and everything," Nikki suggested.

"No, even before the water shortages. Mado says that Pablo is the most superstitious person he has ever met—and that's saying something when you live in Mexico. Pablo believes that evil spirits can lurk in still water, in the well water, but not in running water."

"It kind of makes sense, I suppose." Vanessa said it out loud, even though she was really talking to herself.

"Makes sense to you, Vanessa. Explain, please." Nikki, who was standing behind her, tugged her hair playfully.

"Well, I mean, if you did believe in spirits living in water. The still waters are often murky and can bring sickness to a place, but running water is fresh, so it's healthier. That's what I mean."

"Do you believe in good and bad spirits in water?" Carmen asked her.

"Well, I'm not sure where they live as such, but I definitely believe in good and evil," Vanessa replied stoutly.

CHAPTER 18

Many witnesses report a very bad smell when the Chupacabra is around. It is a strong sulfuric odor that is traditionally associated with *el diablo*, the devil.

On the way home Vanessa avoided all discussion of Pablo and the Martinez family. Instead she told funny stories about her brothers and even got off her bike to mimic Luke's lanky walk and his deep voice. Nikki was an only child and was always telling Vanessa how lucky she was.

"Oh, brothers can be such pains, Nikki, I promise you. You're not missing anything, really—is she, Carmen?"

Nikki laughed and gave Vanessa a playful shove. Later, nobody could recall what actually happened next. Just that Xolo was suddenly there beside them, snarling and growling ferociously, his teeth bared. It took Vanessa a couple of seconds to realize that he was crouched, ready to pounce.

Had Xolo thought Nikki was going to hurt Vanessa? Was he really trying to protect her, as Izel had said? Or was there someone else nearby?

Vanessa tried to follow the direction of the dog's gaze. He was not really looking at Nikki—it was more toward the trees. She saw nobody, but she thought she heard a sound. Footsteps, perhaps? Could it be Pablo? Had he seen them looking at his house?

Vanessa put her hand quickly on the back of the dog's head to calm him. Then she made a low, rumbling noise in the back of her throat, and Xolo relaxed. The moment had passed.

"That's amazing," said Carmen. "The way you can control the dog like that. I thought he was going to savage Nikki!"

"Let's go," said Nikki. "I don't like it here. It's creepy. And there is a horrible smell all of a sudden."

Vanessa patted Xolo, and the dog loped away.

"Race you home!" Vanessa cried, leaping onto her bike again.

"We should have that dog locked away during the day, Joseph," Frida said when she heard the story that evening at dinner. "I have noticed that he is starting to behave erratically."

There was no doubt that Xolo had attached himself to her, Vanessa thought, but that wasn't odd or erratic. He probably never got much affection or attention before, that was all.

"And he needs a wash," Carmen added. "I think he smelled very bad this afternoon."

"The smell wasn't him," Vanessa said flatly to no one in particular. She kept her head down.

There was a slight pause in the conversation, and everyone heard the phone ringing in the hall. It was a surprising sound in the house. It didn't often ring.

Izel arrived, breathless, her face flushed.

"The phone is for you, Vanessa!" she exclaimed as if Vanessa had won the lotto. "Come, come."

The sound of Lee's cool, familiar voice was

wonderful. Vanessa hadn't realized that she was homesick, but now it washed over her without warning. She had to clear her throat a couple of times before she could speak.

"No, no, honestly, Lee, I'm fine. I promise. It's just so lovely to hear your voice, that's all."

Vanessa looked behind her to see if Izel was still with her, but she was alone in the hallway and the door to the dining room was closed.

Lee explained that she had only just seen Vanessa's email, as she had been traveling by train with no access to the Internet. She was in Helsinki now and had rung her straight away, alarmed by the sound of her email.

Vanessa told Lee what she had found out on the Internet about the naguals and the Nahua and briefly went on to explain about Xolo, the dog.

"I'm at my computer right now," said Lee. "I'm just reading here about the Nahua people and their links to the Aztecs. It says they believe that each one of us has a corresponding animal in this world—some good, some evil."

She paused and Vanessa could hear her even breathing on the end of the phone, as if she was standing beside her. It would be so great to have her here. Vanessa was just about to say as much when Lee started reading again.

"Wow, bloodsucking or bloodletting is not uncommon amongst—" She paused. "Just like the Chupacabra, huh? I'm surprised your mum didn't have a file on Mexico, Vanessa."

"She did, Lee—a cryptid file. How stupid of me not to link it all! The file is more about the Chupacabra than the tribes and traditions, I think. I need to read it again properly now that I'm making all these connections."

"Go easy, Vanessa. You could be treading on delicate ground there. It sounds as if things are pretty tense anyhow. Who took you to the shaman's house and the museum?"

Vanessa realized that she had not mentioned Armado yet and did not do so now. Could Armado be involved somehow? Why had he taken her to both the house and the museum when Carmen had been fearful of them both?

When she didn't answer, Lee asked again. "Who took you, Vanessa? Is someone making you uneasy?" It was Pablo, of course—not Armado—who bothered her, but Vanessa couldn't really explain over the phone. And anyway, she didn't want to worry Lee unnecessarily. The less said the better for the moment, perhaps.

"There's nobody, really. I was just freaked, I suppose, by the strange things I saw. Probably the spicy food—Dad did warn me! I'll be all right. I promised Dad I would be, remember? But don't say anything about this to him, will you?"

Lee agreed reluctantly that it was best not to say anything for the moment and then gave Vanessa a number to write down with the promise that she would ring her if anything else strange happened.

CHAPTER 19

In the summer of 2010 over a period of 50 days, 300 goats were killed by an unknown creature. Shepherds from Colonia San Martín, Los Reyes Metzontla, and Cañada Ancha in Puebla State were frightened by the attacks on their flocks, as they were unable to track down the killer.

The next morning Vanessa woke feeling very low. It had been so nice to talk to Lee, and even though she had tried to ignore her words of caution she felt uneasy. It was as if she was waiting for something bad to happen.

Normally Vanessa hopped into the shower as soon as she woke, but this morning she couldn't face the day. She pulled the covers up over her head to hide from it for a little longer.

When the door to her room burst open and Carmen stumbled through with Nikki tripping over herself behind, Vanessa shot up in bed. For a split second she had the brief pleasure of knowing she had been right, but it disappeared quickly at the sight of Carmen, who was distraught.

"Vanessa, it's so horrible!" Carmen wailed.

"Come on, Vanessa, get up," ordered Nikki, throwing Vanessa's dressing gown to her. "You have to come. Everyone is out by the stables. Hurry."

The family was gathered in a tight circle, and Pablo stood off to the side, a shotgun across his arm. A kid goat was stretched out on the ground. Armado was crouching down. Vanessa could see that he had a whining Xolo by the scruff of the neck.

Carmen buried her face in Frida's hair, her shoulders heaving. Frida looked stunned.

"It's Tepin," whispered Nikki. "Carmen's pet goat. He's dead! Those chickens too." She pointed at a heap of feathers on the ground near the dead goat.

"It's extraordinary, I've never seen anything like this before," said a strange man who was washing his hands in a bucket of water. "These animals have been completely drained of their blood. Every last drop."

"That's horrible!" said Nikki in a strangled whisper.

El diablo, thought Vanessa, horrified. *The Chupacabra* . . . Her skin prickled.

"Who's that man?" she asked Nikki.

"That's the vet," Nikki said. "Armado found the goat dead and called him. Xolo was sniffing around him with blood on his face."

Vanessa's heart started to thump wildly.

"You can't really think Xolo had anything to do with it!" Vanessa turned to Joseph, who was standing beside her. "It has to be the Chu—" She made herself stop.

"Well . . ." said Joseph. "There are puncture marks in the kid's neck, and the vet thinks they were probably made by dog's teeth."

"But a dog wouldn't make neat holes," Vanessa argued. Through the fabric of her dressing-gown pocket, she fingered the tooth the turtle-seller had given her. It had to be a very different kind of animal from Xolo. "A dog that killed another animal would tear it to pieces, not drain its blood like a vampire. It doesn't make any sense!"

Vanessa was beginning to shout, and Frida was glaring at her.

"You can't blame Xolo! You just can't. It's so unfair." Xolo was still whimpering beside the dead goat.

Now he looked at Vanessa and tried to go to her, but Armado tightened his grip on the dog.

"Stay," he ordered curtly.

"We just can't be sure, Vanessa," said Joseph. "I think we should lock him up for the moment."

Pablo spat something in Spanish that Vanessa didn't understand, but it sounded threatening.

She ran to Xolo and wrapped her arms around his neck.

"Xolo didn't do it," she moaned to Armado. "You've got to believe me."

Armado touched her on the shoulder.

"We will put him somewhere safe, I promise. In the stable," he said gently. "We will not let Pablo shoot him unless we know for sure it is Xolo who has done this. Do you understand me, Vanessa?"

In the end she agreed to go back to her room with Carmen and Nikki. They were all upset, but they sat on Vanessa's bed together and went over the details of what had happened again and again. Then through the open doors they heard the sound of two shots ringing out. They were loud, even at such a distance, and the girls stared at each other helplessly. Vanessa turned on her side to face the wall and began to cry hard, deep sobs racking her body. Carmen and Nikki did their best to soothe her, but when nothing worked they went in search of Izel.

It was nearly midday before Vanessa woke. She felt as if she had been run over by a large truck, and feebly she put her hand on her chest to check her bruised heart. She would never forgive Armado. He had tricked her, told her that Xolo would not be put down. Slowly she put on a crumpled pair of shorts and her T-shirt from the day before.

The more she thought about poor Xolo, the angrier she got. It was hard to imagine how she would stay on at the ranch now. She would just pack her bags and insist on going home. But what about Nikki? Could she do that to her best friend? Maybe she should tell Nikki about everything that had happened to her since she came to Mexico . . .

Vanessa hadn't realized how much Xolo's devotion had meant to her. The dog had chosen her over everyone else—and she had failed him. The thought of Pablo, his thin lips and cruel eyes, made her feel physically sick now. He had been pretty determined to get rid of Xolo.

Nikki and Carmen were not on the veranda outside or in the sitting room doing their embroidery. Embroidery, for goodness' sake—what a ridiculous place this was!

Maybe ridiculous wasn't quite the right word— what was the right word when shamans go missing, dead people turn into animals and chickens and goats are drained of their blood? And cows had been killed too, Vanessa remembered then. It must be the Chupacabra. No wonder the locals called this place *Rancho del Diablo.*

Vanessa made for the kitchen. She heard the murmur of voices through the closed door. Then she heard Nikki's laugh, and it twisted like a knife inside her. How could she be laughing after what happened this morning?

All eyes turned toward Vanessa when she walked

into the kitchen. Izel was chopping as usual, Carmen and Nikki were sitting at the table shelling peas, and Armado was stirring something on the stove. Cozy. Vanessa's anger was dangerously close to the surface, and it was unfortunate for Armado that he was the first one to speak.

"Hi, there. How are you feeling now?" he asked cheerfully.

She glared at him before answering. "How do you think?" she said rudely.

They all stopped what they were doing, surprise in their faces. All, that is, except Nikki, who was well used to her friend's fiery temper.

"I'm sorry you had to see that," Armado said. "It was a shock for us all."

He spoke as if Xolo's execution was nothing. Vanessa actually saw the color red in front of her eyes just seconds before she replied through clenched teeth.

"As if you had nothing to do with it!" she growled.

"What are you saying, Vanessa? What exactly am I guilty of?" Armado replied, his voice hardened.

Vanessa's face was hot, red hot with anger, and she held his gaze defiantly. She could see that he was puzzled, and this made her more cross. He didn't even realize that he had betrayed her.

"Of being a liar and a traitor," she replied tartly. When he didn't respond she bit her lip, which was wobbling dangerously. She would not cry in front of him. She would not.

"You told me that Xolo wouldn't be put down, you promised me. And then when my back was turned you let Pablo shoot him anyway!"

She just couldn't believe it when a smile started in the corners of Armado's lips and broadened out to a full beam. Then, slowly, to make sure she understood every word, he said, "Yes, I promised you, and I kept my promise."

Vanessa felt the ground shift beneath her and looked about her uncertainly, hoping to catch Nikki's eye. Instead, she caught Carmen's, and her eyes were blazing with indignation. How dare Vanessa accuse her brother! She didn't say a word, but Vanessa could read it in her face.

"But I heard the shots," Vanessa said with a little less conviction this time.

Armado continued to smile at her and there was a look of admiration in his eyes that she really couldn't fathom.

"That was just Pablo taking his anger out on a couple of poor birds," said Carmen angrily. "Mama and Armado would not let him shoot Xolo, so he shot something else. Anyway, he probably should have shot Xolo. That dog nearly attacked Nikki, remember? And now he has killed Tepin!"

"Tepin?" Vanessa was so concentrated on Xolo that she had forgotten the goat's name.

"It was Carmen's kid goat that Xolo attacked," Nikki muttered from the side of her mouth at Vanessa.

Vanessa opened her mouth to defend Xolo again and then shut it when she saw the look on Nikki's and Carmen's faces.

"I think you owe my brother an apology," Carmen said coldly. She looked incredibly like Frida at that moment. "Armado would never go back on his word."

Then Vanessa did something that surprised even Nikki. She walked over to Armado and threw her arms around his neck.

"Did Pablo really not shoot Xolo?" she asked quietly.

"Of course not." Armado hugged her back.

Relief made her rest against him, and she could feel the comfort of his arms around her. It felt so good.

As if on cue, Frida Martinez opened the kitchen door and walked in to a silent room. Her back, which was already ramrod straight, stiffened further. She stared stonily at Vanessa, who stood paralyzed, her arms wrapped around Frida's son.

CHAPTER 20

The world's three species of blood-sucking bats live mainly in the warm climates of Latin America, where most of the Chupacabra attacks have occurred. But while vampire bats can creep up on their sleeping prey, make painless incisions, and lap up the dripping blood, they cannot drain even a tiny animal of all its blood. Animals bitten by vampire bats will occasionally die because they get rabies, not because of blood loss.

It took Vanessa a couple of days to get over her embarrassing outburst in the kitchen. Armado seemed cool about it, but Nikki was still teasing her about throwing herself at Armado. Vanessa tried to laugh it off.

"I could do much better than that dusty cowboy, Nikki. I know he's your cousin and he's nice, but come on!"

She guessed that Nikki didn't really believe her, and she most certainly didn't believe it herself. When Armado was around the air seemed charged around her, and she found it difficult to know what to say. Oh dear. This was not the fun it was cracked up to be.

Frida was a different matter altogether. Vanessa had been mortified by her appearance in the kitchen. If only Frida had said something when she had come in and seen her like that with Armado. Silence and raised eyebrows were far more painful.

Since then Vanessa had studiously avoided Frida. If she saw her coming one way she went the other. Where possible she made no eye contact and no conversation. But she still had the Spanish lessons to face, and they had become a nightmare.

Xolo was no worse for his near-death experience. And although he remained firmly locked away during the night, he was allowed to go out with Vanessa and Armado when they went on their riding lesson. He loved to run alongside the horses as they galloped.

Today Armado and Vanessa took out the horses and headed for the eastern section of the ranch. The sky was a clear, intense blue, and Vanessa's spirits lifted. It was good to get out of the house. Tepin's death had cast a long shadow.

Vanessa had promised herself that she wouldn't bring up the killings. It was too gloomy, and she doubted that anyone would want to hear her theory about the Chupacabra. But when they stopped to let the horses drink from the river, she could not help herself.

"You didn't really think it was Xolo who attacked the animals, Armado?"

It was the first time she'd mentioned Xolo to him since the scene in the kitchen, although it had been bothering her for days.

"Well, he has got a bit aggressive in the last while. He was there when I found the dead animals, and he did have blood on him."

Vanessa took another tack. "But how could he have drained the animals of blood? Wouldn't a vampire bat be as likely? South America is the only place in the world where there are actually real vampire bats."

"Yes but we are in Mexico, Vanessa. It's not the same."

"True," she agreed, though it seemed close enough to her.

"Look, Vanessa, I've seen an aggressive dog on the ranch but not one vampire bat, so on balance . . ."

He didn't finish his sentence, and although he said it playfully it made Vanessa feel a bit foolish. She should shut up.

"But you can't really believe that Xolo could suck every last drop of blood out of two chickens and a goat either, can you?" she said grumpily.

"To be honest, I have no idea what to think, Vanessa."

Armado looked worried, and Vanessa was tempted to say something about the Chupacabra when she was distracted by the sound of a dog barking in the distance. It came from somewhere in the middle of a dense clump of trees.

When Vanessa looked around Xolo was gone. The barking stopped suddenly. Something was up.

Armado and Vanessa looked at each other briefly and then, without a word, dropped down from their horses at the same time and ran to the edge of the trees. Before they could plunge headlong into the foliage, Xolo trotted out beside them looking quite unfazed. Vanessa fell upon him, relieved. He had a bone in his mouth, which he dropped at her feet.

"Silly mutt, scaring us like that," Vanessa scolded him. She picked up the bone. "Thank you for the present, but I've become a vegetarian, I'm afraid," she said to the dog.

"Don't lie to Xolo." Armado patted the dog's head, and Xolo rolled onto his back for a tummy rub. "I've seen you eating your steak—medium-rare—like the rest of us."

It happened then, just as before. An assault on her senses. The same as in the shaman's house, but less shocking, because Vanessa recognized the signs this time. The same foul smell. Vanessa felt as if her eyes were pressed up against a curved glass and the things around her—the trees and horses and Armado— were all distorted. She saw Xolo's head transform into a man's head with smooth, sleek black hair and a hooked nose. Around his small neck was a string with feathers and a large crystal. Beside him was a beautiful woman whose head rotated 360 degrees and became the face of an owl. The bird woman.

Vanessa dropped the bone she had been holding, and Armado picked it up. He had been busy playing with Xolo and had not noticed Vanessa's ashen face. He inspected the bone.

"A deer, I suppose," he said casually and then threw it high in the air back into the trees.

Vanessa turned to hide her confusion. She was shaking. Why was it that she was the only one affected by these visions? Was it some form of message for her, or was her grip on reality just slipping?

CHAPTER 21

Naguals will often hide recently dead or dried animals amongst the belongings of people they wish to harm. Magical manipulations of these animals and the use of potions, incantations, and effigies are used to cause illness and even death.

The next day Vanessa found a dead lizard under her bed.

She was on her knees looking under the bed for her book when she noticed the little dried-out corpse. She wasn't bothered by it; she quite liked lizards. The ridgy skin was so prehistoric looking. Besides, a dead one was easier to get a good look at; the live ones here were way too fast on their feet.

There was no book under the bed, though. It must be in her backpack, she thought. As soon as she opened her bag she knew that something was wrong. Right on top of her things lay a piece of snakeskin and a dried-out frog. The frog was stretched out flat and looked as if it had been hit by a bus. Poor thing. But what was it doing in her bag?

"Yuck," said Nikki, coming into Vanessa's room through the French windows. "What is that in your hand?"

"A dead frog and some snakeskin," Vanessa said flatly. "I have no idea how they got into my backpack. And there was a lizard too, under my bed. Also dead."

"Horrible!" said Nikki.

"More mysterious than horrible, really," Vanessa said. "I don't mind the dead things, but I do mind the idea that someone might have come into my room and left them here."

"Maybe you left your window open," Nikki suggested. "Maybe they crawled in and died there."

"In my zipped backpack?" Vanessa persisted. "And

maybe the dead snake just happened to shed some of his skin as he opened the zipper?"

What could Nikki say?

"Someone put them there, Nikki, and I think I know who."

"You know who?" Nikki repeated with a laugh. "You are beginning to sound like Harry Potter, Vanessa."

Vanessa frowned.

"Sorry. You mean Pablo, don't you?" Nikki stopped smiling and straightened her face. "I know you don't like him, and he is pretty gross, but why would he do that?'

"To scare me again?" Vanessa didn't sound convincing, not even to herself.

"Again?" Nikki echoed.

Vanessa still hadn't told her about the incident in the kitchen, but Nikki was in a hurry.

"I have to go," said Nikki. "Carmen is expecting me. Embroidery. Will you be all right, Vanessa?" Nikki looked hard at her friend. Vanessa was pale.

"I'm fine." Vanessa smiled to reassure her. "I'll see you later."

It was nearly time for Vanessa to go and join Izel

in the kitchen. Maybe she would have an explanation for the dried animals. First she would take a quick look at her cryptid file. She took it out now from the bottom drawer of her wardrobe where she had hidden it amongst her clothes. Since the animal killings Vanessa had been worried about somebody finding it. It was possible that they might suspect her of being involved in some way. They might accuse her of playing tricks. People had been blamed before for the Chupacabra's killings. Somebody was certainly playing tricks on her with the dead lizard and frog.

The first few chapters were about the Chupacabra—the sightings and theories. Vanessa thumbed the pages thoughtfully. She liked to imagine that her mum had done the same, that there was some trace of her still on the paper that Vanessa could connect with.

"What am I missing, Mum?" she said softly.

She could see that the Chupacabra's method of killing was similar to the way the animals had died here, on this ranch. Her next thought made her turn cold: What if it was actually something to do with her, Vanessa? What if she was a key, in some strange way, to the things that were happening? What if the person who left these dead things around in her room knew something about Vanessa that she hardly knew herself?

She sat staring at the pages, her eyes blurry with unshed tears. She was in a panic. She didn't want to analyze it any further, but she was going to have to if she wanted to discover what was going on.

"Help me out here, Mum, will you?" she croaked. She read on. Most sightings had happened in Central and South America, Puerto Rico, and the Caribbean, where it had all started nearly thirty years ago.

Vanessa threw the folder down and gave a loud snort. It was an unpleasant sort of noise even to her own ears, but it was a sound filled with relief. Of course it had nothing to do with her. She hadn't been in Puerto Rico thirty years ago; she hadn't been in Colombia eleven years ago. She'd been overreacting, thinking she might have some unconscious link to the killings. The first attacks on the ranch had happened before she even got here, hadn't they? The most likely explanation, as Armado said, was a wild dog. Just not Xolo.

Vanessa turned the page and got the surprise of her life. There, in front of her eyes, was her mother's handwriting. She ran her fingers over the words and smiled. They were hard to read, more like scribbled thoughts than notes.

The Chupacabra is not just one creature but a type of creature, as the attacks have happened in many countries.

Is it the same thing in each country/place?

Is it a physical manifestation of something evil in a place?

Where do they hide? How can they stay so well hidden and yet leave trails of evidence in the form of dead goats and other animals?

If the killings are the result of a pack of wild, hungry dogs, surely you might expect the bodies to be torn apart by their teeth rather than for the blood to be drunk from three neat puncture wounds?

The word *teeth* made her jump to her feet as if she had gotten an electric shock. The tooth from the turtle girl! Maybe that was the key. She dived into her wardrobe and retrieved her dressing gown, which she had flung onto the wardrobe floor. She rooted in the pockets. Nothing. Had she lost it—or had someone taken it? Someone who had sneaked into her room to leave dead creatures lying about to frighten her? Vanessa went back to the file and read on.

In modern rural Mexico, the term nagual *is often the same as witch or brujos, who are thought to be able to shape-shift into animals at night and suck blood from innocent victims. They can also steal properties and cause disease. In some indigenous societies, the position of the nagual is accepted as part of their community. They may know who the nagual is, and he is both feared and respected for his evil. In other communities the accusation of being a nagual may result in violent repercussions—much like the witch process of renaissance Europe.*

Why had her mother put information about the Nahua tribal traditions in the cryptid file about the Chupacabra? Had she come to the same conclusion as Vanessa? Did she think that the Chupacabra sightings were something much more deep-rooted in Mexican culture—something that went back to Aztec times? Vanessa let the folder drop to her lap. Her head was stuffed full of wild images, but she couldn't quite pin down her thoughts, and she felt quite exhausted by it.

CHAPTER 22

Blood-sucking and transforming witches can be traced back to pre-Hispanic times in Mexico. Locals will often suspect a nagual within a community but would never openly accuse or confront a person, as it is too dangerous. They risk bringing sickness or death to themselves or their family.

"Is *nagual* a Nahuatl word, Izel?" Vanessa asked as she rolled the dough for the tortillas. It was her fourth time to try. All previous attempts had been rejected by Izel—too thick, too thin, and then too dry.

She knew from her mum's file that a nagual was a blood-sucking witch, but she was interested in hearing Izel's version of it. Head down, rolling dutifully, she waited for Izel to reply. When no answer came, she looked up.

Izel's barrel-like body was shaking; the knife that Vanessa had rarely seen out of her hand since her arrival was discarded, and she was holding on to the edge of the counter, as though keeping herself propped up.

"Izel, are you OK?" Vanessa's voice faltered. "I'm . . . I'm sorry."

Izel's mouth was wide open and her many chins had collapsed on themselves.

The word *nagual* came out in a long, slow hiss, rather like the air being let out slowly from a balloon. The army of hairs on the back of Vanessa's neck stood to attention, and she held her breath.

"Never speak of those people," Izel whispered, her eyes wide in panic. "Even that word said into the wind puts you in danger."

The kitchen door opened, and Xolo trotted in, head held high, bat-like ears alert as if he were expecting first place at a dog show. Armado was close on his heels, heading straight into the open arms of Izel, who seemed to make a miraculous recovery at the sight of him.

Vanessa gripped the rolling pin a little harder and resisted the urge to thump Armado with it. That boy's timing was something else. Then a thought popped into her mind unbidden: Was his timing good or bad? Did Armado know what was going on and just act all innocent?

Vanessa stroked the top of Xolo's head as he sat panting by her feet. She was glad to see him out of his lock-up.

"Did Xolo jailbreak, Armado, or has he been given a reprieve?" Vanessa made her voice sound as light and casual as possible. She hated the fact that Xolo was still locked up for much of the day.

"I heard him whining as I passed the stable and felt sorry for him. He led me straight here, though." He grinned at her. "Food. It's a great tempter."

"Maybe he knew that I wanted to ask you something," Vanessa said.

Armado raised his thick eyebrows. A smooth, even tan and mischevious eyes. God, he was good-looking! Vanessa found herself blushing, much to her annoyance.

"Just wondering if the little presents were from you?" she said.

"Presents?" Armado looked amused.

"The snakeskin and dried-out frog in my bag? Or the dead lizard under my bed?" Vanessa replied. "You know, to try and scare me—me being a girl and all that?'

Armado looked really puzzled now; his laugh was genuine, the look of disbelief in his face unrehearsed.

"I would have to put a lot worse than a couple of dead reptiles in your room to scare you, Vanessa."

His smile was friendly, and Vanessa grinned back.

"You know me better than I thought," she bantered lightly and turned to Izel. But Izel had already left the kitchen.

CHAPTER 23

On 3 May 1996 in Calderon Village Sinaloa, Northern Mexico, a giant bat-like creature terrorized the village. Goats were found daily with their blood sucked dry. Farmers formed night vigilante squads. "We are telling people to keep women and children locked up at night," a local said. "Nobody knows really what it is. Dozens of goats have fallen prey to the bloodsucker."

Later that evening the girls ate their dinner at the small table on the veranda outside their bedrooms.

They ate alone. Izel had gone to bed with a

headache, and Frida had not been seen all day. Joseph and Armado had gone to see a well on another ranch that was similar to the one they planned to sink on the Martinez ranch.

Vanessa could not shake the feeling that she was in some way responsible for Izel's headache. She shouldn't have asked her about naguals. Glumly she watched the lizards scuttle along the veranda, their tongues flicking as they collected insects. They had a beautiful blue color on their sides and were about the length of her forearm. Funny, that. The one she'd found under her bed had been much smaller and was just a plain green. Maybe that one was not native to the ranch?

She took a long drink of the cool homemade lemonade. It was delicious and very welcome. Her mind was feverish, as if it were working overtime, cycling repeatedly through all that had happened so far.

"I got a lovely call from home this morning," Nikki said out of the blue.

Vanessa turned to her, suddenly noticing how pretty her friend looked. Nikki's face was tanned and her blonde hair highlighted with natural streaks. It wasn't just that she looked pretty; she was clearly happy, too.

"They sent their love, Vanessa, and said that they bumped into your dad and Lee in Dublin last night. So they went for a drink together and talked about us. For hours, apparently." Nikki paused for a second and then continued. "Mum said that your dad was really worried about letting you go after your last trip to Loch Ness."

Vanessa opened her mouth and closed it like a fish. She didn't really want to go there at the moment.

"What happened at Loch Ness?" Carmen's eyes were trained on Vanessa's face, and Vanessa's heart sank.

"I was stupid. A stupid accident, that's all. I took a rowing boat out on the lake on my own." When Carmen said nothing Vanessa continued. "Then I managed to capsize it and . . . well, I suppose I nearly drowned after I bumped my head."

Carmen's eyes were wide as she listened to Vanessa.

"Luckily I got to the bank before I passed out. It was a close one, I know, but I was fine."

"It must have been terrible, Vanessa. You must have been so afraid," Carmen said. She was not a great swimmer. Vanessa smiled. Falling into the lake and meeting Nessie had been one of the best things that had ever happened to her, but she wasn't about to tell them that.

"Well, it was worse for Dad and the boys because they thought that I had gone missing, and the police were called in," Vanessa said.

"The police were called to find Mama when she went missing," Carmen said. "She was sixteen, and her father pronounced her dead."

"Pronounced her dead?" said Nikki. "How do you mean?"

Carmen shook her black hair off her shoulders; she enjoyed an audience.

"My mother was a very talented artist. Her father was so proud that she had his father's genius, and he planned to send her to study with the best artists in America."

"Oh, yes—his father was the one who carved the dogs," Vanessa said quietly, more to herself, but it stopped Carmen in her tracks.

"Perhaps I'd better not say any more. It is not really my story to tell. It should be Mama and not me."

Vanessa cursed herself and beneath the table she dug her nails into her own palms, annoyed with herself. She could have heard the rest of the story if she had kept quiet. Why, oh why could she not learn to stay quiet and not interrupt people? Her teachers were forever saying it. Now Vanessa had to agree that they were right.

She tried to enjoy the rest of the evening with the girls, playing charades and games of snap with silly rules. But no matter how much she begged, Vanessa could not get Carmen to continue with Frida's story. She remained firm. It was not hers to tell.

At bedtime Vanessa sat on her bed and took out the portrait of Izel that she had attempted and examined it critically. It was pathetic. She couldn't show it to Frida, especially when Frida was an artist herself.

She turned to a blank page in her sketchbook and closed her eyes. The pencil in her palm became the smooth bone she had handled the previous day. In her mind she relived the images that changed and shifted until the woman became the owl. The bird woman. The owl woman, really.

Vanessa opened her eyes, picked up her pencil and began to draw. She did not stop until she had finished. She had drawn the feathers well. But it was the face that really struck her as interesting. The face was that of an owl, but the eyes were the wide, round eyes of a woman. She decided to leave it exactly as it was. She was exhausted.

CHAPTER 24

The Chupacabra has glowing eyes and large fanged teeth. Eyewitness accounts of its color vary from blue-black to lizard green. At some sites where killings have occurred, three-toed tracks were found.

Vanessa thought she heard something beating against her bedroom window. It was a faint but steady beat and echoed dully around the room. Vanessa threw back her bedcovers and walked toward the French windows. She pushed them gently, and they swung open easily. She hesitated for just a second before stepping out in to the night.

The air was thick, the heat intense. Vanessa felt beads of sweat rise like blisters on her skin. She stumbled on into the dark, her hands outstretched as she blindly fingered the air. As she moved, cactus spines scratched her leg and a stone jabbed painfully into the sole of her bare foot. Maybe she should go back, she thought.

Something snuffled and grunted nearby and insects clacked and ticked all around her. In the dark Vanessa struggled to make sense of the sounds and then, through it all, she heard a terrible, high-pitched squeal. She stopped suddenly, her legs like lead weights. She probably wouldn't be able to run away even if she tried.

There was something behind her now. The cracking of a small twig sounded like a gunshot in Vanessa's ears. She turned slowly, forcing herself to look. At first she thought she saw a human face, a face that she knew. But the harder she stared, the farther the face retreated into darkness and another one took its place.

Vanessa found herself looking straight into a large, salivating mouth with razor-sharp fangs.

Above it two glowing red eyes pulsed to the sound of her heart, which pounded in her chest.

Too shocked to scream, Vanessa took off. She didn't feel the cactus tearing her skin this time or the cuts on her knees when she fell. She got up and kept running. Another high-pitched squeal just in front of her finally made her stop. The anguish in the cry echoed her own pain, and her legs gave way. She fell heavily on something. It felt warm and furry and the feel of it repelled her. What was it? An animal? The Chupacabra itself? She squirmed away until she could feel the hard ground beneath her again and then lay still. Total exhaustion overcame her. Instead of leaping to her feet, she lay waiting for the Chupacabra to strike; she could smell him in the air. Vanessa began to shiver uncontrollably.

CHAPTER 25

On 11 March 1995, in the small town of Orocovis in Puerto Rico, locals were shocked when they woke to find eight sheep dead. They had puncture wounds in their necks and chests and had been drained of their blood.

Vanessa woke and found Armado's face only inches from her own. He was whispering, and at first she could not understand his words. Finally they made sense.

"You have to wake up, Vanessa," Armado said urgently.

She smiled at him, relieved to find that it had only been a dream. For a moment she almost felt brave enough to hug him again. She was delighted to feel the soft mattress beneath her. But what was Armado doing in her room?

"Quickly, Vanessa. You have to shower. It's almost light and everyone will be up soon." Armado's voice was brusque, and it jolted Vanessa wide awake. Shower? What did he mean?

Vanessa sat up and looked down at her hands and nightdress. There was blood everywhere. She screamed, but Armado clamped his hand quickly over her mouth to stifle it. He was pressing so hard that it hurt, and she suddenly felt as if she would suffocate. She bit down on his fingers, and he let out a yell. Nursing his hand, he turned on her furiously.

"What are you?" he hissed. "A wild animal?" His face was so close that their noses were almost touching.

The harshness of his words brought her to her senses. She looked at the dried blood on her hands and then touched her cheek. It felt dry and crusty.

"What happened?" Vanessa asked, her voice weak.

"It's all over your face and mouth too," said

Armado. The disgust was easily read in his face. "You don't want anyone else to see you like this, Vanessa. Nikki and Carmen would be terrified. Hurry up!"

It was the mention of Nikki and Carmen that finally got Vanessa moving. She wished she could tear off her filthy nightdress, but Armado was still in the room.

She stared at him, desperate to ask about the dead animal that she had fallen over and whether he had seen the two red eyes, the devil's eyes. Then it occurred to her that it had been the middle of the night. Why had Armado been out? And why had he been the one to find her?

"You'll need to give me the nightdress. I'll get rid of it," Armado said stiffly.

She slipped into the bathroom and came back wearing a clean nightdress. Armado took the bunched-up, bloody one and headed for the door.

He hesitated, the door handle in his hand, and turned back to meet her stare. "You don't look well, Vanessa. Have a shower quickly and then go back to bed. Go on . . . go on," he added gently, shooing her like a dog.

CHAPTER 26

Naguals can cast spells. They use a series of rites, incantations, and effigies. They can put people to sleep and make them lose their will—and, more dangerously, they can cause sickness, fever, and even death.

Vanessa spent the next two days crisscrossing between sleep and consciousness. A couple of times she pretended to be asleep when she heard the door open. She could not face talking to anyone yet. Her mind was a jumble most of the time. She longed to catch hold of a thread that would unravel it all for her.

The doctor visited both days and gave her large white tablets that she found very difficult to swallow. As soon as she put them on her tongue they started to dissolve, and they tasted disgusting.

The doctor was a tall, thin man with wavy black hair that sat in ridges all over his head. It was heavily waxed and didn't move even when he bent down to listen to her heart with a stethoscope. He had a horrible moustache that looked like a giant slug on his upper lip. The rest of his face was nice, though; very crumpled with soft brown eyes that looked constantly amused. He had no English, and Vanessa could not understand a single word of his rapid-fire Spanish. Izel translated for her.

The doctor told Vanessa that she had a very high temperature and the tablets would help bring it down. He said that she was to rest quietly in bed for at least two more days.

Occasionally Vanessa would sneak out of her bed and search the room to see if any other dead animals had been planted. None. She was relieved.

Every time she shut her eyes the image of the Chupacabra loomed beneath her lids. A humped creature that stood half upright. It had enormous fangs, but worst of all were the glowing red eyes. She felt as if she knew those eyes, although maybe it was just the evil in them she recognized.

Izel brought a special soup, which she spooned relentlessly into Vanessa's mouth. It was her own recipe. One she used on her husband when he was sick, she said. Vanessa didn't feel sufficiently well to point out the fact that her husband had died, but she was not so sick that she didn't think it.

Between spoonfuls of spicy soup Vanessa asked Izel if there had been another attack on the ranch. She already knew the answer, but she needed to hear someone else say it.

"Yes, two nights ago, the night you got sick. Four cows this time."

"Well, at least Xolo is in the clear, I suppose. He was still locked up when that happened, wasn't he?" demanded Vanessa.

"Of course," said Izel simply. Clearly she hadn't suspected Xolo either.

"Were there definitely other attacks here before?" Vanessa said weakly. "Before I came, I mean."

She felt Izel's hand cover her own on the bed and

the tears pricked behind her closed lids.

"Yes, *chica*, about four years ago," Izel said. "A long time before you came."

"Then it isn't anything to do with me." Vanessa closed her eyes. The relief made her feel faint. "But why have they started again, Izel?"

"Because something has been disturbed here," Izel replied. "Someone is feeling threatened. The first attack, the one four years ago, that happened just after Frida inherited the ranch."

Vanessa squeezed Izel's chubby, wrinkled fingers. Then she felt a soft kiss on her cheek and smelled the spices that Izel cooked with.

"I do not know, Vanessa," Izel said. "I do not know why these things are. I do not understand what is going on. You're not even Nahua."

Vanessa's eyes shot open. Why did Izel say that?

"Where did Xolo come from?" Vanessa asked instead.

Izel looked surprised. She spooned some more soup into Vanessa's mouth, maybe in the hope of stopping the questions.

"He was Casco's dog before," she said after a moment.

"Casco?" Vanessa asked. It was not a name she remembered hearing before.

"Our shaman," said Izel. "He went to visit his family in the north. Pablo said he would look after Xolo while the shaman was away, but the dog hates him. He would not stay in Pablo's house, so he came to live with us."

When Izel tried to feed her again Vanessa shook her head firmly. Enough of the soup.

"How long has he been gone? Your shaman."

"Many years now," Izel said sadly. "I hope he will come back soon."

"And has nobody reported him missing or sent the police to look for him?" Vanessa asked.

"Patience, Vanessa." The loud bark of Frida's voice made them both jump, and Izel spilt the soup all over the bedclothes. Frida had come in on silent feet. "Sometimes people travel for a long time and then return. It took Joseph twenty years before he went back to visit Ireland, you know."

Frida spoke now to Izel in Nahuatl. Vanessa could not understand a word, but from the way they were arguing she suspected that Izel was standing up to Frida. Their eyes were locked angrily. Then she heard her own name spoken. Spat out by Frida. They turned to her. She felt as if they were waiting for an answer, but Vanessa had no idea what to say. Helplessly she stared back at them, wishing she could close her eyes and be transported home to her own bed in Dublin.

CHAPTER 27

Naguals are frightened by metal. Placing a knife or scissors by the bed or attaching safety pins to a bed sheet or garment at night will help keep them away.

Vanessa fell asleep again. When she woke she could not believe her eyes. Izel was crawling around on the floor. Vanessa watched her through the fringe of her lashes. When Izel gingerly lifted the corner of the mattress at the foot of the bed Vanessa opened her eyes fully.

"What are you looking for, Izel?" said Vanessa. "My folder?"

Taken by surprise, Izel heaved herself to her feet.

"Folder? What is folder?" She sounded puzzled and did not seem at all embarrassed about being caught snooping.

Vanessa pushed herself up onto her elbows and saw a bag on the floor at Izel's feet. It was filled with nails and scissors and long rolls of wire. Vanessa raised her eyebrows. What on earth was Izel up to?

"It is metal," Izel said. The expression on her face was now a cross between sheepish and defiant.

"But what for, Izel?" Vanessa asked.

"To protect you, Vanessa. Those dead animals in your room were a curse. That is why you become ill, feverish. The nag—" Izel stopped suddenly. "It does not like metal." Izel dropped her voice to a whisper and pointed out her handiwork to Vanessa. "This is why I pin safety pins to your mattress and hang nails over your bed."

Vanessa was at a total loss. Did Izel think a nagual had been in her room? The nagual didn't like metal, so safety pins were going to protect her? Vanessa didn't know whether to laugh or cry. It all sounded so silly. But she had to admit that the day she found the animals had been the day she fell ill—and the night that she had seen the Chupacabra. Maybe there was a connection.

Izel handed her a pair of scissors. "It is most important to keep the scissors beside your bed, Vanessa. If you do he will not come near you again. You should sleep now. You must build up your strength for the coming days."

It sounded ominous, but Vanessa simply didn't have the energy to ask what she meant. What on earth had she gotten herself into this time? Her father would kill her.

CHAPTER 28

Lechusa or Le Chusa is a symbol of death in Mexico and throughout much of Latin America. She is a woman who becomes an owl at night to collect souls. When she calls out, those who answer will die.

Vanessa slept the night through and woke the next morning feeling much better. She still didn't want to get up, though. She felt sick again when she thought about meeting Armado and what he might say. What had he done with her nightdress? Washed it? Or burned it? Was it evidence?

She was surprised when Frida sent word via Izel that she was expected at her Spanish lesson today, though she wouldn't have to do her chores. Vanessa would much prefer to have spent time in the kitchen with Izel than have to face Frida. But she got up, as requested, and went to Frida's study with Nikki after breakfast.

Vanessa was shocked at how drawn Frida looked. Her face was closed—the shutters down and locked tight, like a seaside resort in winter. It hadn't seemed possible that Frida could get any colder, but she had.

"I think you are feeling better, Vanessa." Frida didn't give Vanessa a chance to answer. "Did you have time to draw a picture for class before you got ill?"

For a moment Vanessa wondered if she could lie and say no, but she knew that Frida would see straight through her. She opened her sketchbook and handed it to Frida with great reluctance.

"It's not very good, I'm afraid," said Vanessa.

Nikki took a quick peek at it and silently agreed with Vanessa. The feathers were good, but the bird woman's face was all wrong.

Frida stared at it for a long time. For so long, in fact, that Vanessa was beginning to wonder if she was going to speak at all.

"Do you know this legend?" Frida asked, looking directly at Vanessa.

Vanessa felt a wave of terror surge inside her.

"Sorry? What legend?" She shouldn't have drawn her vision. She should have drawn anything but that.

"This picture, it is Lechusa. She represents death," Frida said tersely.

Vanessa stared at the owl on the page, unable to speak. She could feel Nikki's and Frida's eyes burning into her.

"Lechusa is not really an owl but a witch. A winged woman who comes for your soul when you are about to die." Frida's face was expressionless. Her voice was flat and quiet. Her lips barely moved. "If you whistle and Lechusa returns the call, death is near."

"That's a cool story," said Nikki. "It's a bit like our banshee, isn't it, Vanessa?"

It was as if Frida hadn't heard her.

"You can sometimes hear her approach. The sound of her wings will beat in your head."

Now Frida turned to Nikki. "It is said that if Lechusa is captured and forced to see the sun rise, she will turn back into a beautiful young woman. Then she is condemned to death—burned at a stake."

There was a heavy silence when she finished speaking.

"That's a scary one," Nikki said. "But Vanessa loves stories like that. Don't you, Vanessa?"

Vanessa couldn't answer. Frida handed the picture back to her.

"It is well drawn, Vanessa. Now, let us tell the story of Lechusa in Spanish," she said at last.

Vanessa tried her best, but every word hammered on the inside of her head until she thought it might explode. She had no idea what she said.

Afterward, when Nikki asked her about the drawing, Vanessa lied. She told Nikki that she had copied it from a book and didn't like to admit it. She hated herself for being dishonest to Nikki, of all people, but what else could she say? She could hardly tell her the truth. It was just too eerie.

"Honestly, Vanessa, why didn't you just admit that you copied it instead of acting all weird?" Nikki, who rarely got cross, was really annoyed now. "Do you not think Frida and Joseph have enough on their plate without you acting up like that? First there was that scene about Xolo, then you took to your bed for days with some mysterious illness, and now you've lied about a silly drawing and upset Frida even more."

Vanessa was miserable. She wanted desperately to tell her friend about the strange visions and the way things happened to her and not to others. But if Nikki thought she was acting weird now, what would she say if she told her all that other stuff?

CHAPTER 29

Crystals are considered one of the most important objects for a shaman to possess, as they help him to channel his powers.

Things didn't improve the next day either. Nikki and Carmen had paired off. Vanessa could hear them chatting away happily in the sitting room, doing their embroidery. Vanessa was beginning to feel more alone than ever. There was no sign of Armado anywhere, and even Izel had a free afternoon and had gone to visit her sister in the local village.

Vanessa, at a loose end, decided to go and see Xolo. At least he was always happy to see her. She was annoyed that the dog was still being kept locked up for most of the day. He had been in that wretched shed, out of harm's way, when the cows were killed the other night. Obviously he had nothing at all to do with it, so why was he still being treated like a suspect?

Xolo was lying with his head on his paws and only lifted it halfheartedly when he saw Vanessa. There was something wrong.

"Maybe you need a run; do you, Xolo?"

Xolo hopped up, licked her hand and trotted over to the door.

Vanessa laughed. "Well, maybe I really can talk to animals," she said out loud as she pushed the door open.

Her heart all but stopped when she saw Pablo. He had his back to her, but she knew immediately that it was him. There was a long knife in a sheath tucked into the back of his belt.

He turned toward her and stared. He had an axe in his hand and had been chopping wood.

Xolo started to jostle against Vanessa's knees,

almost tripping her up. He was clearly scared. How dare Pablo try to intimidate them like that! She looked at him defiantly and held his stare as she stalked past.

It was then that she saw the string around his neck with a small crystal and three long feathers attached. Where had she seen something like that before?

Xolo growled, a low and rumbling warning. And Vanessa suddenly remembered when she had seen a necklace like that. It was when she'd handled the bone that Xolo had brought to her. Or had it been that time in the shaman's house? What did Pablo have to do with all of this?

CHAPTER 30

El Chupacabra has also been called the Vampire of Moca, the Elemental Beast and Mexican Devil.

It was time to talk to Armado. It had been four days since he had found her covered in blood. Four long, painfully slow days. After breakfast she was going to make a point of finding him and getting to the bottom of this.

Vanessa stood on the terrace and took a deep breath. She loved the sweet scent on the air and the warmth on her face. She put her head back and rested upright against the sun-warmed wall. She loved Mexico despite everything that had happened. Nikki was still being a little cool toward her; she would probably never invite her to Mexico again. Vanessa wouldn't be needed anyway, as Carmen and Nikki got on really well. In fact, Nikki was probably wishing she hadn't brought Vanessa at all.

She found Nikki and Carmen still at breakfast in the courtyard, chatting, and she forced herself to give them a big smile. She sat down and poured herself an orange juice and then bit into a piece of toast.

"The police have just been here." Nikki's eyes sparkled with excitement. "Frida refused to talk to them. It was Joseph who called them in. Apparently they said that it had happened before—the animal killings, I mean. It was—"

"Four years ago and it was wild dogs." Vanessa finished the sentence for her friend.

"How on earth did you know that?" Nikki said indignantly. "And why didn't you tell me?"

"Sorry, Izel told me. I would have said it, only I got sick, remember?"

Vanessa kicked herself. That hadn't helped things

between them. What would happen if Nikki ever found out just how much Vanessa had kept secret from her?

"Have you seen Armado around? He said he would give me another riding lesson once I was better. I'm learning to jump at last," she added hastily, hoping that the word *liar* was not branded all over her forehead.

"Funny, that. He was looking for you not ten minutes ago, although he didn't mention a lesson. Iiinterressting . . ." Nikki drawled the last word for effect.

Vanessa could think of nothing to say, so she aimed the crust of toast in her hand at her friend's head and fled, the sound of the girls' laughter propelling her on.

CHAPTER 31

Curses or magic spells are placed on people with the intention of harming them—causing illness, accidents, and even death. They are the most dreaded form of magic and are universally known as "black magic." Curses laid on families have been known to plague them for generations.

The horses were drinking from the river and Vanessa and Armado were sitting on the bank, cooling down. The tension between them was bad. Vanessa knew they would have to talk about it sometime. They just couldn't keep putting it off.

"Can you tell me what's going on, Armado? I heard the police were here today and that your mother would not talk to them."

"She can't talk about it. She feels that she is responsible," Armado said gloomily, picking up a small stone and throwing it into the river.

Vanessa waited.

"Since she took over the ranch," Armado went on, "four years ago, bad things have started to happen. She believes she has brought the curse here."

"I know this is really difficult for you all." Vanessa paused and swallowed the lump that had formed suddenly in her throat.

"Mama never talks about it. Papa told me a little, but she never has."

"Please tell me, Armado. I need to know." Frida was the key to it all, she felt certain. She just wasn't sure how she had become involved. "You have to trust me," said Vanessa. "Sometimes I see things that other people can't see. I don't know why, I just do."

She could see that he was thinking. He looked into her eyes. Then he pushed away a strand of her hair that had fallen across her face and tucked it behind her ear.

"I will tell you what I know. Although I know Mama would hate us talking about this." He got up and began to pace the bank just behind her, his hands in his pockets.

"She was about sixteen when Papa moved into the house. My grandfather had hired him to be my mother's tutor. When he found out that they had fallen in love, he went mad. He locked her up in her room for weeks at a time. Nobody was allowed to visit. My father was thrown out of the house. He was lucky to have made it out alive."

"How did they get back together then, to get married?"

"Months later my mother ran away, I don't know where, but she went to him. Her father sent the police after her, but they did not find her. They married in secret. That's all Papa ever told me. The rest I picked up from Izel, and I've tried to piece the story together."

"I see, but what about the curse?" said Vanessa encouragingly.

"Izel told me that Don Miguel, my grandfather, put a curse on Frida and swore that she would never set foot on the ranch again. He made sure that she wouldn't inherit the ranch when he died. It went to a nephew instead, but when that nephew died suddenly, he left it in his will to Frida, so she inherited it indirectly. That was four years ago."

"Ah," said Vanessa. "So that's why she thinks she has brought the curse to the ranch. She went against her father's wishes, even after he was dead. And maybe that is why she puts up with Pablo now. She's trying to put it all right again and lift the curse."

Armado looked surprised. "I'm not sure. I know Pablo was close to my grandfather. So maybe you are right. If she does right by him . . ."

Vanessa nodded. "Izel believes that it was Pablo who told Don Miguel about Frida and Joseph's love affair. She says that Pablo poisoned the family against Joseph."

"She never told me that," Armado said.

"OK," Vanessa said. "So let me get this straight. Four years ago your mother inherits the ranch and you all come to live here. Things start to go bad straight away: animal killings, drought, the ranch starts to lose money. Also four years ago, the local shaman goes missing and supposedly leaves Pablo in charge. But why does Xolo, the shaman's dog, hate Pablo? And why does Xolo act like a guard dog to me?" Vanessa stopped and frowned.

"And what about you?" Armado said quietly. "Why did I find you out in the middle of the night, lying beside a dead cow, covered in its blood?"

The question, finally asked out loud, made Vanessa wince. She didn't dare raise her eyes to meet his. Instead she put her hand in her shorts pocket and felt the shrunken head. The words came out of her mouth before they had time to form in her mind.

"Because I am a threat to him." Suddenly she understood. "I saw him that night, Armado. Pablo is a nagual. I know, because I saw him transform—into the Chupacabra."

"Nagual? Chupacabra?" Armado was shocked, but Vanessa could see that he still didn't believe her. "Slow down, Vanessa."

"Speed up, more like it! I've only just put two and two together. But I definitely saw his face, and then I saw the face of that horrible creature—the fangs, the red eyes. He knows that I know about the murder too."

"Murder? Vanessa, what on earth are you talking

about now? I know it was horrible, but it was only a cow."

"I don't mean the cow, Armado," said Vanessa. "Come with me."

CHAPTER 32

Current theories about the Chupacabra include the belief that they might be aliens, vampire bats, living dinosaurs, and even the result of genetic mutation experiments that have escaped from a government laboratory.

"Where to?" Armado asked. "Back to the ranch?"

"Yes. To get Xolo." Before Armado could ask why, Vanessa said pleadingly, "Just trust me, please, Mado. I have to show you. It's too complicated to explain." They went and got Xolo, and the dog ran with them alongside the horses. He seemed to know where to go, and as soon as they reached the forested area he disappeared once again into the trees. After a moment he reappeared with the same bone he'd brought to Vanessa a few days previously.

"This is like déjà-vu," said Armado as they dismounted and tied up the horses. "What is this all about, Vanessa?"

Xolo rubbed up against Vanessa's leg and gave a sharp bark. Then he turned and walked briskly in amongst the trees. Vanessa followed closely on the heels of the dog.

"Where are you going now?" Armado sounded alarmed.

She didn't answer him, just kept following Xolo. Armado had to run to catch up with them.

After about ten minutes they came to a small clearing. Xolo began to scratch and scrape the ground in the center. Vanessa watched at first, and then she knelt down beside him.

"Vanessa, what are we looking for?" Armado asked, but Vanessa was too busy clawing at the dried earth to answer.

"Vanessa?" he asked, sounding frightened.

"Just help us dig," she ordered.

They found a second bone. Armado picked it out of the soil and cleaned it off. He held it out to Vanessa, but she refused to touch it. She wasn't going to make that mistake again. Distracted, she examined her hands. Her fingernails were caked with red clay, and two of her fingers were bleeding. She was shivering slightly now.

"A shallow grave," she said grimly.

"A grave?" Armado was shocked. "It's not what you would call a grave, Vanessa. It's just a bone that Xolo buried so he could dig it up later. It's his stockpile. He's a dog, after all. They do that."

"It's human," Vanessa said adamantly.

She had seen enough bones in her lifetime, because of her mother's interest in archaeology, to know the difference.

Armado said nothing for a moment. Then he seemed to change the subject. "What were you doing out in the dark, Vanessa? When I found you the other night, I mean."

Vanessa struggled to articulate the words. She felt sick.

"I don't know. I was sleepwalking and yet it was real, too."

"The blood was real," Armado said quietly. "It was all over your face, Vanessa. You looked like a vampire."

"The cow, the one that was killed, I stumbled over it in the dark, fell on top of it, face down. That's all." Armado didn't answer.

"It's got something to do with all of this," she went on. "I know it, Armado. The bones, the curse, the Chupacabra. They're all linked."

"The Chupacabra?" Armado did not hide the incredulity in his voice this time. "Come off it, Vanessa. You can't honestly believe in that nonsense, can you? Isn't the Chupacabra meant to be an alien from outer space or something?"

As he said it Vanessa's certainty evaporated. Maybe she was talking nonsense. Maybe she was barking totally up the wrong tree.

"Just dig, will you?" she said crossly. "There'll be more bones, you'll see. I'm telling you, it's a grave, Armado. I can't touch the bones myself," she explained. "That's why you have to dig. Last time I saw terrible things." She tried hard not to let her voice sound tearful. "But I suppose you think that's a bit loony too."

Armado didn't reply. Why was she the only one seeing things? It wasn't her ranch, not even her flipping country.

The next bone they found was definitely not from an animal. It was undoubtedly a human femur with the funny angular ball part near one end of it.

When Armado measured it up against his own upper leg it was clear that it had come from someone about his size or a fraction taller.

Vanessa still did not touch it. She sat cross-legged on the ground and said, "See? How tall was the shaman?"

Armado's eyes grew round in disbelief.

"I don't know," he said. "He left not long after we moved in, I think. I didn't know him."

Vanessa waited for him to come to the same conclusion as she had herself.

She could see that Armado was beginning to doubt himself. He looked deeply troubled, and now he began to dig frantically. Xolo whined gently beside Armado, his head resting on his paws.

"But who would do such a thing?" Armado

shouted as he dug up another clearly human bone. "Who would bury someone here?"

The answer hung in the air between them.

"A murderer," she said quietly at last.

"Oh God." Armado had found the skull. "Murder." He exhaled he word at last. "But why?"

"Evil," Vanessa said. "*El diablo*. Whatever you want to call it."

"But the shaman was a good man," said Armado. "The people respected him."

"Yes, but Pablo wears a crystal and feathers," said Vanessa. "I am sure they belonged to the shaman." She spoke calmly, feeling sure of herself now.

"I still don't understand," wailed Armado.

"When Frida inherited the ranch, it was under the protection of the shaman," Vanessa explained. "But there was a curse on Frida, remember? Your grandfather had cursed her."

"You mean the curse killed the shaman? That doesn't make sense."

"No, listen. The shaman protected the ranch so the curse could not take effect. The only way to make the curse work was to get rid of the shaman."

"Right," said Armado. "And who wanted the curse

to take effect? You say Pablo because he has the shaman's beads."

"Feathers," said Vanessa. "And a crystal—a kind of necklace, a charm, I suppose."

"That proves nothing."

"Pablo wanted to be in control of Frida's downfall," Vanessa said. "That's why he killed the shaman. Once the shaman was gone, Frida and the ranch were no longer protected. The curse began to work and things went from bad to worse. Animals attacked, drought . . ."

There was a wild look in Armado's eyes. He grabbed Vanessa's backpack and put the skull into it. Then he took her firmly by the hand and pulled her to her feet.

"Quick, we have to tell Papa and confront Pablo." He looked around suddenly. "For all I know he could be hiding and watching us. I caught him outside your room the other day. Maybe he had been inside your room, now that I think about it. The door was open a fraction."

"Dead lizards and frogs," Vanessa said ruefully. "I thought he just meant to frighten me, but . . ." Armado looked puzzled. He didn't remember immediately.

"Pablo planted them to put a spell on me, to make me sick, to stop me finding out the truth. I'd say he has an effigy of me with pins in it, too." She stared coolly into Armado's chestnut-brown eyes.

"You probably think that's all rubbish, but Izel believes it. She put metal safety pins around my bed to protect me because naguals don't like metal."

She paused for a moment. "You still don't believe me, do you? I can't—"

"Stop, Vanessa!" Armado interrupted her. "We don't have time now. We have to hurry back."

CHAPTER 33

The Aztecs believed that xolo dogs were needed by their masters' souls to help them safely through the underworld. Today the xolo breed is still sold in rural Mexico for its meat. It is believed to have extraordinary curative powers. It is sold on the black market and is strictly against the law.

It took a while to round up the family and Izel in the kitchen.

Vanessa insisted that Armado tell the story— a very abbreviated one, leaving out the curse and

Chupacabra and focusing entirely on the murder.

When Armado produced the skull, their story finally started to become real.

Frida took the skull gently from Armado and held it reverently in her hands. Then she turned to Vanessa.

"I always suspected Pablo had something to do with Casco's disappearance. Casco was a good friend to me when I was young. Thank you, Vanessa," she said. Frida's eyes glistened, and Vanessa wondered if she was going to cry. Wow, this really was another side to her. But Vanessa had not been part of the storytelling and was surprised that Frida was saying this directly to her.

"Oh, but it wasn't me," she said. "It was Xolo, really. He's Casco's dog," she added when she saw their blank faces. "He attached himself to me from the moment I arrived here, remember? He wanted to tell me something from the very beginning, only I couldn't work it out at first. He was the one that led me to the bones . . . the body."

It took a couple of hours for the police to arrive and get spotlights set up. They dug as darkness fell. The noises of the forest and the nighttime insects began to fill the air and Vanessa tried to hide her growing frustration. Why didn't they go straight to Pablo's house to arrest him? They could always continue digging in the morning when it was light.

When she said as much, Joseph's gentle reminder that evidence comes first did nothing to calm her. As they waited, Xolo sat at Vanessa's feet, and Frida stood close to her but made no attempt at conversation. Vanessa had two protectors now.

For the next few days the police came back and forth to the ranch, digging more holes in the clearing and asking questions. By the time they pieced the story together and went to Pablo's house, it was no surprise to Vanessa that Pablo had fled.

There was no need to break in. They simply opened the front door. The policemen went first, followed by Joseph and Frida and then Armado and Vanessa. Carmen and Nikki had stayed back at the house with Izel, who said she could not prepare all the meals without help.

As they shuffled forward into the room, the stale smell was the first thing to hit Vanessa. She heard a sharp intake of breath from Frida, and when she finally got into the small room and looked around she was horrified to see a load of dogs lying on the floor. They were all hairless like Xolo. Some were lying on top of each other, others on their own. None were moving.

"Oh my God!" Vanessa cried. "They're all dead."

"No." Joseph put his hand on the chest of one of the dogs. "The brute. He's drugged them."

Looking closer, Vanessa was relieved to see the small rise and fall of the dogs' chests. She looked at their black hairless skin. They were like Xolo, but there was something different about them. They were much bigger, and their heads were a strange shape. One or two had their mouths open, and Vanessa could see that their teeth and gums were deformed.

"Why did he have so many dogs?" Vanessa asked. One of the policemen looked at her and answered in Spanish.

Frida translated for Vanessa. "Pablo was breeding the xolos for meat. Some people around here believe it cures sickness and protects against evil." Frida sat down on a bockety chair. "The xolo was a sacred dog for the Aztecs, and they ate the meat all the time. I was given some of it as a child."

Frida fell silent. Vanessa tried not to let her disgust show on her face.

"It's illegal now, of course," Joseph added, "but it is still sold on the black market." His voice was grim. "Big money. That was what Pablo was after, obviously."

"But why do they look like this? Their faces all deformed, their teeth such a mess?" Vanessa asked tearfully.

"It's probably inbreeding," said Joseph. "If you keep breeding from within a very small group of related dogs, you get deformities."

"Oh, how could he do that to those poor dogs?" Vanessa was upset now. "Izel was right. He is *el diablo*," she said bitterly.

"They all seem to be alive, at least." Armado put a reassuring hand on Vanessa's shoulder. "My guess is that they have been drugged to keep them quiet most days. He probably exercises them at night."

"He exercises them at night all right..." Joseph said angrily. "On my livestock! It is these deformed creatures that have been killing our cows and goats. Look at their teeth."

"Well, at least all that is over now," said Armado. "Thanks to Vanessa."

Joseph put an arm around her shoulder and smiled

grimly. "Mystery solved. I must say it is an enormous relief."

Vanessa looked at Frida, who had said nothing since she'd told them about being fed dog meat as a child. She seemed to have aged ten years by simply crossing the threshold of Pablo's horrible house. But she didn't look upset now, or distressed, Vanessa thought; she looked distracted. Or maybe bewildered was a better description.

CHAPTER 34

In Mexico, naguals or blood-sucking witches are believed to experience an uncontrollable craving for blood as many as four times a month. But June, July, and August are the rainiest and coldest months, and this is when naguals are most active.

The last couple of weeks of Nikki and Vanessa's stay were very pleasant. The dogs had been taken away by the vet, and there was no sign of Pablo. He had stolen one of the horses and appeared to have gone for good.

Frida and Joseph were in much better moods, and

they made a huge effort to entertain the girls and to put the terrible business of the dogs behind them. They went on shopping trips to the beautiful towns of Quértaro and San Miguel de Allende and visited the famous old silver mines. Frida told them stories of how, as a kid, she used to climb down the mine shafts with her friends and then swim out by the river.

They were beginning to see what Frida must have been like as a carefree young girl. She had even taken to riding with Armado and Vanessa on the occasional evening before dinner. Mealtimes had improved too, more chat at the table and much more laughter.

A couple of evenings before they were due to leave, Izel made an even bigger dinner than normal—a banquet in the girls' eyes—in honor of their departure. They were already making plans for Carmen to visit Ireland next summer, although they were still unsure if Frida would allow it.

"Get Armado to come with you," Vanessa suggested eagerly.

Nikki and Carmen exchanged a knowing look, and Vanessa felt her face burning. This blushing thing was becoming an absolute nuisance. She never used to do it.

That night as she lay on her bed, Vanessa's mind went back to the evening that they had found the dogs. She didn't believe that the dogs were responsible for killing the livestock, but everybody else seemed to. Everybody but Frida, perhaps. She had looked confused rather than relieved.

She remembered the creepy feeling in Pablo's house—damp and smelly. It had literally been a prison for those poor dogs. She thought of the sink in the kitchen that was piled high with dirty plates and wondered if they were still there. The place was a testament to a dismal and lonely life. She didn't feel sorry for Pablo, however; it was hard to feel sorry for someone who had killed another man, a good man, a man who only wanted to help the local people and protect the family.

Besides finding the dogs, the thing that had surprised Vanessa most about Pablo's house had been the paintings. While there had been almost no furniture, apart from a small table and chairs, there was a series of delicate watercolors in clip frames on the walls. It was very difficult to imagine that Pablo was in any way artistic. Even if he hadn't painted them himself, it was still a surprise to see them there.

Vanessa finally fell into a light sleep around three o'clock in the morning, waking again about two hours later. It was still dark outside but she felt wide awake, her mind super alert and her heart thumping. He was back; she knew it. The killings would start up again.

She got dressed, slipped quietly out of her room, and made her way along the corridor to where she thought Armado's bedroom was. She had never been there, but she had seen him disappear into it a couple of times.

Standing there looking at three identical doors along a wall, she froze. What if she picked the wrong one? After a few moments of indecision she knocked gently on the first one. There was no response, and she stood with her clenched fist poised to knock again. Maybe she should just go on her own. But her memory of the last time she had come face to face with Pablo in the dark was not one she could easily forget, and she found herself knocking again.

It was Frida who opened the door, however. She did not appear in the least bit surprised to see Vanessa, though Vanessa's toes curled with embarrassment in her flip-flops. She mouthed an apology to Frida and backed away.

But it was as if Frida had been expecting her.

"Let's go, Vanessa," she said decisively. "We'll take the horses."

Vanessa didn't ask herself why Frida was fully dressed. She just allowed herself to be led through the back door and out to the stables.

They had saddled up their horses and were riding in the direction of the river before Frida spoke again.

"I assume you were intending to go to Pablo's house. How do you know that he has come back to the ranch?"

"I don't know how. I sometimes just follow an impulse when it comes to me. Maybe it's not always the best thing to do, but . . ."

Frida smiled. She understood.

"I ran away with Joseph on an impulse," she said. "But would I go back and change it—even with all that has happened? Lose Carmen and Armado? Never."

Frida shook her head vehemently, her long hair cascading down her shoulders. It was the first time that Vanessa had seen it out loose. She looked much younger, like a teenager, really.

Frida rode slightly ahead. When they got near

Pablo's house, which was still in darkness, they slowed down.

"Did you notice the paintings on the walls in Pablo's house?" Vanessa asked. "Did he paint, do you know?"

"They are mine. I was shocked to see them. I always thought that my father had burned them along with the rest of my belongings, but Pablo must have saved them from the bonfire."

Why would Pablo, of all people, want to save Frida's paintings?

They tied up their horses not far from the house, but out of sight, and made their way on foot. Frida didn't knock; she walked right in and turned on the light. The room was exactly as before. Nothing moved, and no sign of Pablo. Vanessa examined the paintings.

"They're beautiful, Frida. So delicate."

They sat on either side of the rickety table and waited.

A few birds began to sing as the darkness lifted slowly outside, and then finally the door groaned on its hinges. Vanessa jumped in fright and glanced quickly across at Frida. She looked calm and very poised.

Pablo had his large curved knife already in his hand, and Vanessa kicked herself for not remembering it. What had they walked themselves into? They were sitting ducks.

He barely glanced at Vanessa. His eyes were trained on Frida. For a split second, Vanessa saw the pleasure in his face at seeing her and understood at last: Pablo had been in love with Frida all his life. When she chose Joseph without a moment's hesitation, his love had turned him inside out, and he'd sought revenge upon her. First he had destroyed her relationship with her parents, and now he was destroying her ranch.

Pablo spoke intensely, the knife resting on the table between them. Vanessa could not understand a single word of it. Nahuatl, not Spanish. His voice started low and soft, pleading, but when Frida argued back he began to gesticulate, pointing to the ground where his dogs should have been. He was getting really angry, but Frida did not appear to be backing down. Oh, God, how would this end?

Pablo grabbed the knife and stuck it into the table, making it stand on its point. Frida never flinched, but Vanessa shrank back in her chair. She could hear the blood roaring in her ears. It was her fault. Why on earth had she brought Frida there in the middle of the night?

In fact, it was no longer night; dawn was almost upon them. Outside Vanessa heard a bark—a low, clear bark that she recognized instantly.

"Xolo," she gasped.

She watched, horrified, as Pablo turned to her and his face broke into a sickening leer. His bottom teeth were blackened and many of them were missing. But it was the glimpse of a single, huge, sharp tooth in the upper row that shocked her to her core. Pablo rose to his feet, opened the door, and whistled loudly.

Vanessa jumped to her feet too, in panic, ready to run out to Xolo. "No!" she shouted loudly. "Leave Xolo alone!"

Frida grabbed Vanessa by the shoulders and held her close. Vanessa shook her off angrily.

"He's going to kill him this time. We have to stop him, please," Vanessa begged.

"Let him go," Frida said quietly. "Trust me, Vanessa." Her voice was barely above a whisper.

Another whistle from Pablo was followed by a bark. This time it was closer, and Vanessa shut her eyes. She couldn't bear to think of Xolo dead, drained like the others.

"Listen," Frida whispered.

Vanessa focused on the noises outside, every muscle in her body waiting in terror to hear Xolo in pain. And then she heard it, the faint hooting of an owl that grew louder, the beating of wings. Lechusa?

She pulled away roughly from Frida, determined to stop Pablo.

"It is Lechusa, Vanessa. The owl woman. But it is Pablo's call she has answered. Her wings beat for him this time and not for you." Her tone was urgent.

Vanessa was rooted to the spot, her eyes wide with terror. Lechusa? It was only a myth, a legend . . . wasn't it?

They waited in silence until the day broke. When they went out into the dawn, there was no sign of either Pablo or Xolo.

CHAPTER 35

Felix Martinez Hernández, president of Colonia San Martín, said that on 14 August at around 7:00 a.m., over 36 goats were found butchered in the Colonia San Martín strip, located 11 miles south of the municipality. He said that the presence of a predator, nagual, or the Chupacabra was suspected.

Nobody else was up yet when Vanessa slipped back into her room. She was heartbroken over Xolo. She wondered how much of the story Frida would share with the rest of the family—as little as possible, she hoped. What if her father found out? He would put her under house arrest for the rest of her life if he knew the half of it. And what about Nikki? Vanessa knew that it would be very hard for her friend to understand.

She need not have worried. Nobody mentioned a thing all day. Their last day on the ranch passed normally—well, as normally as possible—until Xolo suddenly reappeared.

Vanessa was ecstatic to see him. After close investigation she found a few deep scratches on his neck.

"He must have been fighting with one of the other dogs," Nikki remarked when she saw Vanessa cleaning the wound.

"I will get some . . . what do you call it in English? Oh yes, disinfectant," Carmen said. "We must also check the others."

None of the other dogs had a scratch. To Vanessa's relief, the matter was forgotten by Nikki and Carmen in a matter of minutes.

She wondered if Pablo was still lurking around. Or was it possible that Lechusa had really come for him? Certainly the atmosphere on the ranch had changed. Maybe the killings would be over now.

On the last day Vanessa dressed in her travel clothes. It felt odd to be in jeans and runners after months of T-shirts and flip-flops. Joseph and Carmen were going to make the trip with them to the airport. Izel hugged them warmly and gave them each a beautifully wrapped package in a banana leaf tied with string.

"Some of my special cherry brandy fool cake for the journey," she said proudly. "I will send you the recipe, Vanessa. In the post. Watch out for my letter." Frida hugged Nikki warmly and gave her a couple of beautiful Spanish storybooks. "Keep up your Spanish lessons, Nikki." She patted her affectionately. Frida turned then and smiled at Vanessa. She placed a small canvas into her hands. Vanessa looked at it in surprise. It was similar to her own picture of Lechusa but much, much better. Instead of pencil it was done in watercolors. The feathers were extraordinarily detailed and the colors beautiful.

"I have decided to go back to my painting properly next year, once the ranch is back on its feet," said Frida. To Vanessa's immense surprise, Frida leaned forward and kissed her on both cheeks. "Thank you," she said, dropping her voice.

Vanessa threw caution to the wind, then, and put her arms around Frida's shoulders, hugging her hard. "Thank you for putting up with me. I was a terrible guest, really."

Frida laughed. "You must both come again." Armado was the only one who had not come to see them off. Vanessa didn't want to point the fact out, but she could not leave without saying good-bye to him. While she had really enjoyed the last week, swimming and sightseeing all together, riding with Armado alone had been the best.

Vanessa stowed her bag in the boot of the car and then put her presents from Izel and Frida carefully on her seat beside her. She kept her head down, trying not to show how put out she was that Armado hadn't made an appearance.

"I wonder where Armado is?" she finally muttered to Nikki.

Nikki looked surprised. "I saw him about eleven o'clock and he said good-bye to me then. Didn't you see him?"

Vanessa was shocked at how painful her disappointment was. Tears welled in her eyes and she blinked rapidly to make them disappear, all too aware that Nikki was staring at her miserably.

The car pulled out onto the driveway, and they made their way slowly down the avenue for the last time. Vanessa and Nikki waved to Izel and Frida through the back window. It seemed more like four months than four weeks since they had arrived.

They approached the huge metal arch that stood on its own, marking the entrance to the property. Vanessa looked at it with a heavy heart. It had seemed so odd to her when they first arrived, but now it was entirely normal. She would miss Mexico.

Out of nowhere the sound of hooves thundered. Vanessa was the first to spot Armado.

Joseph pulled up and waited patiently while Vanessa got out to say good-bye to him. Nikki had already said good-bye, so she just waved from the back seat.

"Promise to come with Carmen to Dublin next year," Nikki called out through the open door.

Vanessa stood with her back to the car, unsure what to do or say now that the moment had come. She put out her hand to shake his, but when he caught it he turned the palm upwards and brought it to his lips. It was the gentlest of sensations, yet it quite literally took her breath away. Vanessa said nothing in the end, just turned and got back into the car. Her face said it all.

As they drove back toward Mexico City, a tremendous rainstorm hit them at about midday. Big fat drops sounded on the car roof. When they stopped at a gas station, Vanessa and Nikki bought Cokes and stood in the rain. They clinked their bottles in a toast to the Martinez ranch, delighted at the thought of the water stores filling up at last.

CHAPTER 36

Science has so far failed to explain the physical evidence that has been found—puncture wounds, draining of blood, sometimes dozens of animals dead in a single night. Pathologists at the National University of Nicaragua studied the corpse of a dog-like creature that locals claimed to be a Chupacabra. After many tests and much delay, they finally reported that they could not identify the species.

Izel's letter with the recipe arrived in Dublin not long after they arrived home. To Vanessa's surprise, a newspaper clipping also fell out of the envelope. She unfolded it and read:

Strange Happenings on Rancho Del Diablo

There has been a series of livestock killings on the Martinez ranch in the region of Guanajuato. Some locals have claimed it to be the work of the Chupacabra, but now the mystery has been solved by the police. The deaths of chickens, goats and cows are understood to be the work of a pack of dogs which were being bred illegally on the ranch. The famous xolo meat was being sold on the black market.

Vanessa shook her head vehemently. Dogs, nonsense! Then she read on:

The man who was responsible for the breeding of the dogs, and thus indirectly the killings, was ranch hand Pablo Sanchez.

In a bizarre turn of events, he himself was found drowned when the river near his house burst its banks after heavy rains. The police are treating his death as accidental. His is the third death in the region due to

the heavy floods in recent days. No foul play or mys-
terious creatures are suspected by the police, but the
local man who found Señor Sanchez's body says that
an extraordinary giant tooth was found in the dead
man's pocket.

Mysteriously, the school of veterinary science in
Mexico City has said that the tooth does not belong to
any known creature in existence.

Vanessa laughed out loud. There were times since she returned home that she had wondered if she had imagined the whole thing. She had only told her dad and her brothers a very skinned-down version— no naguals or Chupacabras—but she had told Lee everything.

Vanessa read the newspaper article again. It was a relief to think that she had been right all along. Pablo had stolen the tooth from her room. It was the tooth that had first alerted her to the existence of naguals and led her to the discovery that they could trans-form into the Chupacabra. And no wonder Pablo had gone to such lengths to steal it back. A nagual him-self, he certainly wouldn't have wanted her to have evidence like that!

But Frida had been right too—Lechusa had come for Pablo that night.

Vanessa wondered how many other naguals were still out there, and a quick shiver ran down through her body. At least there was one less Chupacabra in the world.

NOTE

In Mexico, the terms *nagual* and *nahual* mean the same thing and are both pronounced *na'wal*. They come from a Nahuatl word meaning "disguise" and are human beings who can turn themselves into animal forms. I chose to use the word *nagual* in this book as it was less easily confused with Nahua and Nahuatl, which refer to the people and their language.

ACKNOWLEDGMENTS

Lots of people helped me in so many different ways with this book.

Siobhan Parkinson and Elaina O'Neill in Little Island have once again been the stars—guiding, pruning, nurturing, and making the whole publishing process a fantastic experience and my book a better book. Thank you so much.

Thanks again to my writing buddies Paula, Gemma, Una, and Geoff for their much needed encouragement. To Jenny for her help with the

Spanish words in this book, but really for the years of friendship, and Debs for always being at the other end of a phone for me.

But none of it would have happened without my children, Callum, Myles, and Oliver, my mother, Mers, and husband, Ian, who are my number one fans.

REFERENCES

I am indebted to a wide range of books and Internet sites that I used when I researched and wrote this book. I cannot possibly list them all but the following are a great source of information about the Chupacabra, naguals, and Mexican myths and legends.

Cryptozoology A to Z: The Encyclopedia of Loch Ness Monsters, Sasquatch, Chupacabras and Others by Loren Coleman and Jerome Clark

Blood Sucking Witch Craft by Hugo G. Nutini and
John M. Roberts

*Shamanism: An Encyclopedia of World Beliefs, Practices,
and Culture, Volume 2,* edited by Mariko Namba
Walter and Eva Jane Neumann Fridman

www.cryptomundo.com
paranormal.lovetoknow.com
www.cryptozoo.monstrous.com
www.paranormal.about.com
www.themystica.com
www.mythicalcreaturesguide.com/page/Nagual
en.wikipedia.org/wiki/Nagual
www.britannica.com
www.lasculturas.com

ABOUT THE AUTHOR

Dr. Jean Flitcroft started her career as a script writer for medical and scientific films and later became a travel writer when her obsession with travel won out. It was on these journeys around the world that she started writing books for children. She lives in Dublin, Ireland, with her husband and three sons. Learn more at www.jeanflitcroft.com.